I0687518

Framed

by

Nikki Andrews

This is a work of fiction. Names, characters, places, and incidents are either the product of the author's imagination or are used fictitiously, and any resemblance to actual persons living or dead, business establishments, events, or locales, is entirely coincidental.

Framed

COPYRIGHT © 2014 by Nikki Andrews

All rights reserved. No part of this book may be used or reproduced in any manner whatsoever without written permission of the author or The Wild Rose Press, Inc. except in the case of brief quotations embodied in critical articles or reviews.
Contact Information: info@thewildrosepress.com

Cover Art by *Diana Carlile*

The Wild Rose Press, Inc.
PO Box 708
Adams Basin, NY 14410-0708
Visit us at www.thewildrosepress.com

Publishing History
First Mainstream Mystery Edition, 2014
Print ISBN 978-1-62830-243-1
Digital ISBN 978-1-62830-244-8

"Were they lovers?"

Jenna asked, wide-eyed. "You always hear that about artists and their models." Then she blushed.

"Oh, no! Jerry never had any interest in her as a woman."

"But they died," Jenna prompted, absorbed in the story.

Ginny nodded. "Ten years ago last winter. They went missing during a snowstorm. The police went nuts trying to find them. At first, everyone assumed they had just run off together, but it wasn't like that. Mike, her husband, really stirred things up, insisting something had happened. He forced the cops to look into it.

"It took the authorities about three weeks to find them. A hunter came across them in the snow." She looked rather sick. "The coyotes had been at the bodies, but it looked like he killed her and then himself. Mike moved out west and never came back."

She sighed and returned to the present. "All of which means you may have a gold mine on your hands, Jenna. Let us clean it up, verify it is what I think it is. There may even be a signature under all the grease and smoke. Would you feel better if we came up with an agreement about what happens then?"

Sue and Elsie excused themselves and went to the workshop down the stairs from the gallery. "I'd forgotten he killed himself," Sue said.

"Don't you believe it," Elsie replied. "Jerry wouldn't hurt a fly. That was no murder/suicide. It was a double murder."

Praise for *FRAMED*

"I didn't want to put it down."

~Julie MacShane, author

~*~

"Couldn't help myself—stayed up till 2 a.m. to find out whodunnit."

~Pat Lynch

~*~

"*FRAMED* is a really fun read, lots of suspense and some wonderful characters in a novel setting."

~ Jessie Salisbury, journalist and romance author

~*~

"Andrews immediately moves her reader into an intimate knowledge of rural New England, where three would-be sleuths take their friendship to its limits in order to solve what may be the crime of the season."

~Destine Graf, M.A. English and American Literature

~*~

"A gem of a cozy mystery."

~Diane Breton, editor

Dedication

For Dave, who believes in me

Chapter One

The second snowstorm in two weeks bulged down out of Canada, threatening to close roads all across New England. Yaneque Duprey hoped it would hold off a couple more hours so she could finish her deliveries before the state police closed the highway over Temple Mountain. At the moment, a mean, nasty rain of small hard drops hissed on her windshield. Some of the drops were ice. Not a good sign.

Yaneque took justifiable pride in her new business, RunAround—"Let us RunAround for you!" A lot of people had tried to discourage her from offering the courier service, but back when she was still in high school running errands for her family and neighbors, she saw a need in the scattered little towns of southwest New Hampshire. It wasn't long until she figured out a way to fill it. She ran regular pickups at the drugstore for the senior citizens' homes, worked out a deal with a grocery store to deliver orders, and made herself available for packages that needed quick, personal service. She'd started small, with a beat-up old car she nursed along until she could afford a brand new PT Cruiser with her company logo painted on each side. Now, several years later, all the licenses and insurance had fallen into place and Yaneque had regular runs along the Keene-Mill Falls corridor. She was on her way to the Great American Dream—but snowstorms were a nightmare.

Why Jerry Berger chose today to call RunAround for a special delivery, she couldn't imagine. All her other accounts understood about the weather, sometimes even phoning her to tell her to stay home. Not Jerry. He wanted this package out today, before noon, if you please. She assumed it was a painting; Jerry was an excellent artist with a widening reputation. She sighed and tucked a wayward braid under her knitted cap.

He'd better have the item packaged and ready. Today's errands required four trips over the east-west Temple Pass, twice in each direction. Jerry's errand would take her to Westford, near Mill Falls, where she would pick up a parcel for another client and run it west beyond Keene, practically to the Vermont border. At least Berger hadn't quibbled about the mileage and fuel surcharges, the way her other client had. Jerry was like that; she didn't hear from him for months, then he would have a rush job for her. This time was exceptional even for him, though. He wanted this item picked up and delivered so fast that on a good-weather day she'd have had to push the speed limit. Well, her contract allowed for weather delays. And she wouldn't let him waste her time with his usual badgering about modeling for him.

Yaneque switched on her wipers and headlights as she downshifted for the last climb up to the old ski resort. Truckers coming toward her from the west flashed their four-way blinkers in warning. Snow whipped from the roofs of their trailers. She gritted her teeth and hoped her snow tires were all the sales rep had promised.

Spitting snow mixed with the rain by the time she got to Douglass, where Jerry lived and had his studio, just below the Temple Pass. In the distance, clouds shrouded the peak of Mount Monadnock and its long ridge wore white far down its shoulders, where it had already been snowing for some time. Maybe Temple Mountain would hold the storm to the west, as it often did. If the storm didn't cross the pass, she could do Jerry's errand and get home before the road closed, postponing the Vermont trip until tomorrow.

Jerry was pacing impatiently outside his door when she arrived. He clasped a paper-wrapped parcel under his arm, and his intense blue eyes were cloudy with worry. "Hey, Jerry!" she called as she lowered her window. "What's the hurry on this one?"

The artist thrust the package at her with paint-stained fingers. He was in no mood for conversation. With none of his usual warmth he snapped, "Can you make it to Westford with this weather? I hear it's gonna be bad."

She set the small parcel on the seat beside her and held out a clipboard for him to sign. "Do my best, Jerry. It's getting icy on this damned dirt road of yours. Why do artists always have to live back of beyond?" She shut her lips on the words. She hadn't meant to open a conversation, not with this weather. He usually loved to talk about his work.

Not today, however. He shrugged and cast a worried eye down the road. "Cold out here. Gotta run. You be careful. Call me when you get to Westford, will you? I won't rest easy 'til I hear it's been delivered."

"Sure," she said, feeling uneasy. Berger looked very nervous. Pale, even. His fingers twitched and he bit at his lip. "You okay?"

"Touch of the flu, maybe. Go...go now before they close the pass." He stepped back and made shooing motions as she negotiated a three-point turn in his muddy driveway. She really didn't want to mess up her beautiful new car.

By the time she reached the highway, the snow was flying thick and fast. With every stroke of the windshield wipers it packed into a deeper mass, and they labored to deal with it. Yaneque turned up the heat and directed it to the windshield to try to melt some of the heavy, wet stuff as it built up. She passed one refrigerated truck that had abandoned the effort and parked on the side of the road in one of the little areas cleared between banks of snow for just that purpose. The PT Cruiser held steady on the climb, but with every couple of feet that she rose, the snow came down harder and visibility dropped. She was nearly on top of a logger before she spotted its four-ways blinking. She slowed to let him gain some distance.

As they crept up the road, Yaneque caught sight of the blue flashers of a state police car ahead. At the same moment, she realized no one was coming down from the other direction, and she gulped. The cops must have already closed the mountain westbound, and she would be the last car allowed in the pass eastbound. If only there were no cars strewn across the road on the east side, she might make it yet.

Jerry's parcel had better be damned important!

The logger made slow but steady progress up the last steep incline, and Yaneque continued to hang back. At the top, on the very short level space before the road dove into the next valley, she pulled over to catch her breath. She shook with strain. A state trooper, his face blue with cold, peered into her window.

"You okay, miss?" he asked, clenching his teeth to keep them from chattering.

"Just taking a breather, Officer. Is it bad down below?"

"Road iced up real fast, and then with the snow on top, we're having to close it 'til we get a salter up here. I can't let you stay long, or you'll never get down."

She nodded. "Right. I'll be fine. Take care of yourself."

He stepped back and she put the car in gear, careful not to spin the tires. She felt the slipperiness under her as she regained the pavement. It was harder than ever to see.

The logger was already invisible in the thickening storm. Yaneque eased down the road, straining her eyes for any sign of the shoulder. Earlier traffic had churned a single lane in the middle of the road. She stayed in that as much as she could, but conditions were all but a whiteout. She thought the road should bend a little to the left just about here, or was it a little farther on? She peered through the shrinking cleared space on the windshield.

Without warning, a huge black mass loomed up out of the snow in front of her. Automatically, she slammed on the brakes. The rear of her Cruiser spun toward the shoulder; the front wheels jolted into something long and hard and Yaneque lost all control of the car. She had just an instant to realize the logger was jackknifed across the highway. She careened toward him at a ridiculous speed—how fast had she been going anyway? It couldn't be this fast! Then she slammed into more logs. There was a sensation of flipping over. The airbag exploded in her face, and something hit her head very hard.

Damn, I'll have to paint the car again.

Everything went black.

****

When Yaneque came to several days later, she couldn't make her mind work very well. Eventually, she remembered setting out from her house that morning and feeling proud of her Cruiser—totaled, demolished, gone to the crusher, the nurses told her, relieved at her narrow escape—but she never recalled anything else. When she heard Jerry Berger and one of his models had been discovered dead in the snow miles away, she mourned the loss of a client but never connected him with her accident.

In time, the insurance paid for a new PT Cruiser. Yaneque got her logo painted on it and soon she was back on the road. Sometimes when she drove over the pass, she wondered if her memory would ever come back. As the years went by and her business grew, she ceased to worry about it. Most people would be happy to forget what she couldn't remember.

Chapter Two

Ten Years Later

"He stood on the *stepladder?*" Sue and Elsie screamed with laughter. The rickety old ladder they used to change light bulbs would provide dubious support for someone of Jim Hatcher's heft.

"Just so he could see his framing?" Elsie Kimball asked.

Ginny Brent nodded, grinning. "I put it on an easel for him, but he just couldn't picture it, so he had to stand on the ladder and have me put it on the floor—mats, frame and all. Then he sort of swiveled his hips so he could see from different angles. I thought the darned thing would fall over."

The three women stood gathered around the design table at Brush & Bevel, Ginny's art gallery and frame shop. It was a cozy place with warm, butter-yellow walls and clear lighting. Samples of artwork decorated the walls. All the classic media—oils, watercolors, and photography—were represented, as well as high-quality prints and unique mementos like a christening gown and some old crochet. The display changed on a regular basis, creating a moveable banquet for the eyes.

"Honest, you two would've been in hysterics." Ginny laughed now, too, releasing the giggles she'd had such a hard time restraining while the customer was in the shop.

Sue Bradley looked at the print lying on the framing table, a photo of a classic train thundering over a trestle at night. "And it took you an hour to put a black mat and a black frame on this simple poster?" she asked in disbelief. "What else could you have put on it?"

"Well, some of the grays would do," Ginny replied. "But you know Jim. He just couldn't make up his mind which black. Then he couldn't decide on the margin size. We spent half an hour arguing whether it should be two and a half inches or two and three-quarters. Then it was the frame. Once that was settled, he got hung up on which glass to use!"

"You showed him the samples?" Elsie asked. She noticed the display of glass samples sitting next to the print—conservation, non-glare, and museum quality.

"Of course I showed him. Naturally, he loved the museum glass."

"Naturally," her employees chorused. They high-fived each other for their simultaneous response.

"Museum glass is practically invisible," Elsie added.

"And three times as expensive," Sue noted. In unison, she and Elsie rubbed their fingers together in the classic sign for money.

Ginny sat down, her pique at the customer fading. "You two are a regular comedy routine." She chuckled. "What do you think he said then?"

"How much?" they chorused again, and giggled.

Sue thought he would have declined to use it, but Elsie disagreed. In her opinion, Jim Hatcher would have taken the expensive glass just for the snob appeal.

Ginny crowed. "You're both wrong! He liked it so much he claimed he ordered it the last seven times he was in here!" Her annoyance flared up. "Now, don't you think that if we'd sold him seven pieces of museum glass in the past, we'd remember it?"

"With our memories, maybe not," Sue joked. "No, seriously, we haven't ordered museum glass in months. It's great stuff, but just too expensive for most people."

Ginny looked at her two employees, the best team she'd had in her twenty years in the business. The three of them worked beautifully together, their strengths and weaknesses complementing and compensating for each other. Elsie, generous with her time and energy, tall and quiet but prone to rare and delightful outbreaks of silliness, always did a thorough job of thinking things through before she did them. Sue, more volatile, had a paradoxical ability to focus on a job at hand and get it done despite distractions. Ginny knew without vanity that she was a good businesswoman, with a flair for marketing that kept the customers coming in. Between them, Brush & Bevel almost always delivered framing orders on time and perfect, while attracting new business and generating repeat orders.

"So what are you going to do?" Elsie asked, sobering down from their giggles.

"You're *not* going to change the glass on his previous orders," Sue vowed. "Not without charging him for it."

"Of course not. We'll just wait a few days to let him think about it, then we'll go over the glass with him again just to be sure he understands it. Don't worry, I'll handle him."

"Good. I'd probably bite his head off."

"You probably would." Ginny chuckled, knowing Sue as well as she did. "Let me take care of him. I'll tell him it looks perfect with the conservation clear."

Sue snorted in derision. Elsie touched her finger to her nose and then stretched her arm straight out in front of herself, a gesture that recalled Pinocchio and the effects of his tall tales. "Nosy gals, that's us."

Ginny shook her head, smiling. "It's not a lie. It does look perfect. I just have to convince him it does. I'll pull up his old work orders to show he never ordered museum glass before."

"Better you than me," Sue conceded. "Call me when he comes in. I want to see how you manage this."

The doorbell rang, and they looked up to see a stranger walk in. Elsie rolled up the train photo with its work order while Sue put away the mat and frame samples to clear the design table.

Ginny greeted the stranger. "Hello, how can I help you today?"

The woman, well-dressed and, judging by the expensive jewelry in her ears, having no reason to worry about money, shook Ginny's proffered hand. "I'm Jenna Rudolph. I've just moved here from Boston, and this oil painting needs to be cleaned. My new neighbor recommended you."

"Let's see it." Ginny gestured to the now-cleared table. "We do that kind of thing all the time."

Jenna produced a paper-wrapped parcel from the large shopping bag she carried. "My husband bought this at an auction," she explained. "It used to hang in a bar he liked when he was single, down on the Cape. Anyway, the bar went out of business and auctioned off a bunch of stuff, and my husband bought this. It's filthy, what with all the smoke and such."

As she spoke, she unwrapped it and laid it face down on the table. It was a stretched canvas, without a frame, the wire attached directly to the stretcher bars. The wooden bars were warped and showed signs of mold, and the canvas had loosened over time. "We can remount it," Ginny began.

"Oh, I don't know if it's worth that," Jenna objected. "I just want to get it cleaned, then we'll see." She turned the piece over.

It was a landscape, a small one. A few large rocks in the middle of a wood, the glimmer of a lake barely visible through the trees. Just off-center, partly screened by one of the rocks, a nude woman looked over her shoulder at the viewer. Her hand extended to the right. "I hate it," Jenna said, "but Bob likes it. Can you finish it by the end of next week? It's our anniversary."

Ginny ignored her. Her eyes ate up the image, and her mouth hung open. Her words floated out on a long, soft breath. "My God. It's a Jerry Berger."

Chapter Three

Sue and Elsie peered over her shoulder. Of all the artists Brush & Bevel featured, Jerry Berger was their favorite. They never got tired of his work, of matting and framing his prints or admiring either of the two original canvasses the gallery housed, or the several at the Sullivan Museum in Mill Falls. Ginny worked for the Berger estate as the agent and publisher of his body of work, keeping it before the public and taking a cut of the profits. She couldn't have run the gallery on what she earned from his work, but it was a nice chunk of change.

"Are you sure?" Sue touched the edge of the canvas with tentative reverence.

Ginny only nodded. She couldn't trust her voice. Jerry had been a friend, too, long ago. She reached out for support to the very stepladder that had occasioned such hilarity a short time ago. "Oh, Jenna," she sighed.

The woman took a chair on the opposite side of the table and looked at Ginny in surprise. "Is it valuable?"

Ginny looked up with tears in her eyes. Elsie pushed a chair behind her and she sank into it. "I don't know yet," she managed, after a brusque clearing of her throat. "He has a national reputation, and an unknown work by him could be extremely valuable. Especially this one. He completed only one other nude that I know of, and this one is much, much better."

Sue repeated her question. "Are you sure this is his work? I mean, it looks like his, but then I'm not trained to recognize authorship."

Elsie touched her arm. "This is his work all right." She indicated the woman in the painting. "That's Abby Bingham. She used to be a customer. She never modeled for anyone else. Oh, it was a long time ago! Jerry pestered her for a year 'til she finally agreed to sit for him. And then they died."

Sue's mouth made a round O and her eyes went wide. "That's right! I didn't work here then but I remember hearing about it. A murder/suicide, wasn't it? In a snowstorm?"

Jenna gaped at them. "You mean this painting has a story? And it was just hanging in a bar? How the heck did that happen?"

Ginny wiped her eyes and found her voice. "I don't know, but I'd really like to find out. Abby told me she was going to sit for him again, but I never heard any more about it. When they died—" Her voice dropped off.

Sue laid a hand on her boss's shoulder. "Tell us the whole story, Ginny. I remember some of it, but Jenna doesn't know it."

A long moment passed while Ginny collected her thoughts. Then she began, "A long time ago, oh, twenty years at least, Jerry came in here with some of his paintings. He was better than average, so I arranged a show for him, sold some of his prints. We became friends. He kept getting better and better, and we found a better printer for his work. We had unveilings here, too. I remember when he showed *A Walk in the Rain* for the first time. It was stunning, the way he captured the sun just coming out at the end of a thunderstorm. That was the one that really earned him some attention. He won prizes for it. After that I didn't see him as much, because he started to work with a regional publisher. But he would stop in now and then to show me a new painting, or we framed something for him. He was always so full of ideas, and so enthusiastic. Like a kid at Christmas every time he had a new work coming out.

"Then one day he came in when Abby was here. I don't remember what she was doing, probably framing some art for her husband's office. Jerry stared at her like he'd just seen the Mona Lisa or something. He was usually rather shy, but he just blurted it out, asking her to sit for him. She said no at first, her husband wouldn't like it. Jerry told her to bring her husband along, he wouldn't mind.

"Well, after about a year she agreed to model. Jerry showed me some of his drawings of her. He'd pose her as a Victorian lady, or in riding clothes, things like that. At first, he was just practicing his figure drawing. Later on, he got more daring, draping her in silk or brocade, until they worked their way to sheerer fabrics. I don't think either one of them planned on nudes, but they gradually got more comfortable with each other, until one day he asked and she said yes."

"Were they lovers?" Jenna asked, wide-eyed. "You always hear that about artists and their models." Then she blushed.

"Oh, no! Jerry never had any interest in her as a woman. I think he thought of her as a doorway into another expression of art. He was getting bored with landscapes, you see, even though he was so good at them, and he wanted to move into something else. Which basically means figure painting. Abby had no interest in him either. He was—something she did, kind of an experiment. She was like that, always wanting to try new things. She couldn't have kids, so she would adopt projects. I think Jerry was a project of hers. They got along fine, but they weren't lovers. Not that I could ever tell, anyway." She fell silent again.

"But they died," Jenna prompted, absorbed in the story.

Ginny nodded. "Ten years ago last winter. They went missing during a snowstorm. The police went nuts trying to find them. At first, everyone assumed they had just run off together, but it wasn't like that. Mike, her husband, really stirred things up, insisting something had happened. He forced the cops to look into it. He even came in here, didn't he, Elsie?"

"Oh yes, I'll never forget that day. I came in at nine as usual and went down to the workshop. When I came up here at ten to open the gallery, there he was, sitting there with a gun on his lap in the dark. 'Where is she?' he shouted. 'You set her up with that artist, and now she's gone off with him!' I was afraid he was going to kill me!" Her eyes were dark with remembered fear.

"That was before I started working here," Sue explained to Jenna. "Ginny got the alarms put on the door because of him."

Ginny resumed the narrative. "It took the authorities about three weeks to find them. A hunter came across them in the snow." She looked rather sick. "The coyotes had been at the bodies, but it looked like he killed her and then himself. Mike moved out west and never came back."

She sighed and returned to the present. "All of which means you may have a gold mine on your hands, Jenna. Let us clean it up, verify it is what I think it is. There may even be a signature under all the grease and smoke. Would you feel better if we came up with an agreement about what happens then?"

Clearly, Ginny wanted to talk to Jenna in private, so Sue and Elsie excused themselves and went to the workshop down the stairs from the gallery. "I'd forgotten he killed himself," Sue said.

"Don't you believe it," Elsie replied. "Jerry wouldn't hurt a fly. That was no murder/suicide. It was a double murder."

Chapter Four

Sue Bradley drove to work the next day with her windows wide open, singing at the top of her lungs. She thumped the steering wheel in time with Queen's soaring guitars. The sun shone, the maples were in bloom, and the air was sweet with the scent of fresh-turned earth and new-mown grass. On a day like today—her song faltered and the sun dimmed.

Six years ago on a day like today, some nameless fool of a driver, fiddling with a radio perhaps, had drifted into oncoming traffic, jerked at the wheel, and gone his merry way down the road. An ordinary, careless act, one that happened daily on every highway. Except this time Peter, her own heart's beloved, had swerved to avoid the fool and ended up in a ditch, then in an ambulance, and finally in the morgue. On a day like today, with a bright sun shining and the birds filling the air with song, her world had shattered.

Her mourning had been deep and intense. When she emerged from it a year later, she had made a determined list of her remaining blessings. Peter had left her comfortable, though far from rich. She had a fine son and a strong daughter, a cozy home—oh, so empty now!—and a job she loved. She was quite aware that Ginny and Elsie had carried her through the year. She was grateful for their understanding. They'd given her the demanding physical labor to keep her busy and

17

tired out, and let her get on with her grieving. The pain she'd thought would never leave eased bit by bit until it was no more than a remembered sorrow. Yet at times it could still pierce her like a needle to the heart.

The fool had never been found. Sue didn't care; what difference would it make? Peter would still be dead. She had trouble sometimes recalling his face, but now and then, she could feel his arms around her and hear his last words. "See you tonight. Love you."

Sue squared her shoulders and wiped her eyes. It was still a beautiful day, and she had work to do. Best to focus on what lay ahead. She turned off the highway into the parking lot of the refurbished old mill building that housed Brush & Bevel.

Besides the art gallery, a number of other businesses occupied the ground floor: a deli known as The Silver Spoon, a restaurant called the Chowdah Bowl, and Jemmie's Gems. Sue waved to the fishmonger's driver delivering the catch of the day to the Bowl and exchanged pleasantries with one of Jemmie Demarais' jewelers. Jemmie himself was a thorn in the side of all the other tenants of the building, including Brush & Bevel, but the men and women who did the jewelry design and production were nice enough.

The Silver Spoon was doing its usual brisk morning business as commuters stopped in to pick up coffee and maybe a sandwich for lunch. A constant flow of customers went in and out at lunchtime, too. The Chowdah Bowl was always full with midday diners, but it really came into its own at the supper hour. Locals came for a dinner out or a takeout order. And while they waited for a table or for their meals to be packaged, they would look in the windows of the gallery at the beautiful prints and originals hanging on the walls.

As Sue unlocked the door of the gallery, she nodded to the small, shy woman taking the first of her numerous cigarette breaks on the covered walk in front of the stores. The woman worked in one of the offices on the second floor of the building, which now boasted brand new elevators in addition to the wide, restored staircases.

Rather boring but necessary things went on upstairs: an insurance company, some sort of bank, and a medical-supply order center. The refurbish was not yet complete on the remaining three floors, but rumor had it there would be medical offices, a spa or gym, and perhaps even some residential condos. The people who worked in the offices ordered chowder or sandwiches now and then, but otherwise they kept to themselves, except for the cigarette woman. She smiled and waved as she paced back and forth before the windows, but she spoke little English and didn't encourage conversation.

Sue slipped through the door and keyed in the alarm code. When she'd first begun working here and Ginny had given her a key, she'd walked in one morning and completely forgotten the code. Thirty seconds later, the sirens had blared, lights flashed, and within a minute, she was explaining herself to the police. Fortunately, Ginny vouched for her as soon as she arrived, but Sue had acquired a healthy respect for the security system and an abiding confidence in the local cops. A theft at Jemmie's was handled with equal dispatch. All in all, Brush & Bevel was as well guarded as could be arranged, short of iron bars on the doors.

While the computer booted up, Sue flicked on the accent lighting and did the other routine things to get ready for the day: she started the CD player, checked the cash drawer, and turned off the answering machine after listening to the messages, which consisted of two hang-ups and a "Sorry, wrong number." She fixed a pot of coffee and then pulled up the gallery's website on the computer, clicking through to the information on Jerry Berger.

She scrolled through the thumbnails of his works: *Autumn Glory*—a blazing orange sugar maple, *Cape Cod Ladies*—old Victorian houses, and *Vermont Hillside*, all so familiar to her from the prints that still sold at regular intervals. She lingered over his earlier pieces, like *Fire and Ice*—an early snow on autumn leaves, *Birch Meadow*, and her favorite, the *One Year* series. This was an ensemble of four paintings of a toppled but not-yet-dead beech tree as it coped with the changing seasons. She often wondered where the tree was and if it still lived, or had been sawn up and carted away from its place on the edge of a meadow. Berger's paintings of it traced the beech's struggle to survive. She thought it significant the series began in the fall. Despite being blown over by a windstorm in late October and looking rather tattered through the snowdrifts of winter, the tree grew pale green leaves and catkins in the spring, and by summer, it sported a full head of glossy leaves. It looked healthy, even strong.

A painter who captured such a will to live so vividly would never commit suicide.

Yesterday, Elsie had insisted Berger's and

Bingham's deaths were murder, but then things got busy and they never got back to talking about it. Sue looked forward to a good chat with Ginny.

As she prepared to head to the workshop in the basement, a UPS truck pulled up in front of the gallery. A fresh-faced young fellow, not their regular driver, carried a long, heavy box into the shop and held out his pad for Sue to sign.

"I wasn't sure where the delivery door is in this building," he began, but Sue doubted that. There was a large sign directing trucks to the back of the building, where a service lane provided access to the receiving area. Some of the delivery people tried to avoid going back there, where they would have to actually carry packages a few steps.

"It's downstairs and around back," she said, ignoring the pad. "I'll show you." She gathered up her belongings and a framed piece so her hands were full, leaving the driver to carry the box.

He sighed, but followed her down the steps.

"The one drawback to working here is this dreary basement," Sue commented. "On the other hand, we can open the doors and let the sun in on nice days. You can get to all the businesses through here. There's a freight elevator over there at the left end. That will take you upstairs. This regular door is usually open by eight for the food deliveries. You can open the garage door if you need to. Just make sure you close it before you leave. Here, this is our workshop." She unlocked a door marked with the gallery's logo. "Please knock if the door is closed. There are three rooms in here and sometimes we might not hear you come in."

"Why, you get scared?" he asked, just short of

sneering.

"We've had an armed intruder," Sue replied without fuss. "We don't like to be surprised." That should shake his attitude, she thought, and it seemed to do the job. He held out his pad again, and this time she signed it. Then she relented a bit and walked him to the big garage door. She opened it to the surprising view of a pretty little park and the river beyond it. "Some of the delivery people come here for their lunch breaks. There used to be another mill back there by the river, but it burned down a long time ago. The city razed it and put in the park."

The driver's face softened into a smile. "Thanks." He held out his hand. "I'm Jason, by the way. I'm taking over this route."

"Sue Bradley. Just make sure you're not blocking the lane, and nobody will mind if you park back here. But make sure you close the door if you open it."

Since his truck was parked out front, Jason went back up the stairs and through the gallery. After checking that he knew the way, Sue entered the workshop, listening for the doorbells that would tell her he'd left. She heard a clatter of footsteps in the stairwell and Yaneque's cheerful hello as she made a delivery to the insurance company. Sue called back, but continued with her routine.

The tracking board on one wall of the shop indicated where each project stood in the timeline. Sue made a list of the frames that needed to be joined, and then pulled out the frame pieces for the week's deliveries. Carefully, she unwrapped each set of legs from its foam package and scrutinized the cut mouldings for flaws. Once she was satisfied with the quality of the wood, she labeled each frame with the customer's name and colored the cut ends so the raw wood would be hidden at the seam. There were only seven frames today. She should be able to get them done before lunch and spend the rest of the day doing the final assembly.

FedEx delivered two more boxes of frames, and the beverage truck dropped off several dollies of sodas for the Silver Spoon and the Chowdah Bowl. Just before ten, Sue sighed and went out to remind the trucker to close the double-wide garage door. Jemmie habitually arrived at ten. If the door was open, he would have a fit. Sue and Elsie would have liked to open that big door to let in fresh air and sunshine, but Jemmie had a horror of "critters." Although the landlord had installed a screen that kept out the bugs, Jemmie insisted mice and chipmunks and frogs—he really had a thing about frogs—would get in somehow and chew on the door into his storage area. No one could convince him frogs were more likely to seek out the moist places in the woods than the bare cement of the basement, nor that any rodents that got in would head straight for the food storage areas. No, he insisted, the door had to remain closed. Whenever he heard the door mechanism working, he rushed downstairs to supervise the delivery and close the door as soon as it was done. Then he would inspect his storeroom for signs of frog chewing. His employees welcomed these daily absences from the jewelry showroom, but they were a major annoyance to everyone else.

The overhead door was still open when Sue went upstairs to unlock the gallery, but it was closed when she returned. Jemmie was in his storeroom, muttering about frogs. Sue ignored him and got on with her job.

****

Ginny arrived a short time later and called down on the intercom to announce her presence. "Come up when you have a minute," she suggested. "We need to talk about the Berger painting."

Sue didn't exactly rush the joining of the frame she was working on, but it didn't take her long to put it together. She grabbed her coffee mug and climbed the stairs again.

"Good morning," she said with a cheerful smile. "I was hoping you'd say that!"

Ginny tidied up some papers on her desk and waved Sue into a chair. "I see you were looking at Jerry's page on the website."

Sue, who had left the page up on the monitor, nodded. "I couldn't remember if you had any biography on him, or if it was all just his prints."

"I just mention he died ten years ago. There was no reason to mention the circumstances."

"Especially if it was murder."

"It was suicide," Ginny corrected her. "The police all said it was a murder/suicide. It's best to leave it at that."

Sue knew her boss pretty well by now, having worked with her for nine years and more. "That's what the police say. Looking at his work I wouldn't have guessed it, and Elsie said yesterday it was murder. What do you really think, Ginny?"

The older woman sighed. "I knew Jerry Berger for ten years. He was excited about life, happy in his work. Suicide is sometimes hard to predict, but I just don't see it in Jerry's case. But the police were so sure."

"Did they find a note?"

"Not that I ever heard of."

"Tell me what you remember," Sue urged. "Tell me everything. When did you first hear about it?"

Ginny considered. "You know, I thought about it all last night, trying to get it straight in my head. I think the first thing I heard was that Abby was missing. It was in the papers, I know that, because she went missing the day of the big snowstorm that December. It was a nor'easter, we got about forty inches of snow on the coast and a lot more inland." Ginny grinned at her exaggeration. "Well, okay, it was probably about ten inches on the coast and about sixteen inland, if I remember right. Mike Bingham was frantic, as you might imagine."

"He's the one who scared Elsie so much, sitting here in the dark with a gun in his lap," Sue prompted.

"Yes. Well, that happened about two weeks later, I think. After they found Abby's car at Jerry's place. Nobody thought to look there at first, from what I remember. I mean, she wasn't scheduled to go there for a sitting. They checked all the hospitals and police reports at first, thinking because of the storm maybe she was out someplace and got hurt. Then they checked with her relatives and friends, even though Mike insisted there was nothing wrong between them, to see if maybe she left him after a fight."

"Had they been fighting?"

"Not according to Mike. According to him, everything was hunky-dory."

"You sound doubtful."

Ginny shook her finger at Sue. "Don't you go putting words in my mouth," she scolded, only half-serious. "I don't know anything."

"But you suspect something."

Ginny sighed and her half-smile faded away. "You know how you get a feeling? Sometimes when Abby came in here, I thought something was wrong. She was sad a lot. But then I put it down to not having kids. She would've been a great mom." Her eyes focused inward as she looked back in time. "One time she said something about adoption, but Mike didn't want kids who weren't his. I wish I could remember exactly. After that, she began taking on projects."

"Like what?"

"Oh, she did a lot of things. She started the garden club in Westford, and then she got the elementary school to plant a garden. She worked on getting land set aside for conservation, sponsored a boy from the high school to go to a special leadership training course. Things like that. Things to improve the town, help people out. She was in the Big Sister program for a while."

"But she and Mike never adopted."

"No."

They sat for a moment. Sue was about to ask another question when the door opened to admit a customer. Ginny sat up straighter and shot a quick glance at Sue. "Hello, Sunny!"

Though Sunny had been coming to Brush & Bevel since her teens and was now in her early thirties, her taste had not improved. She was a prolific spender, very friendly—and very high maintenance. She always needed special attention and tended to take days to make up her mind on a framing job, only to change it again a week later. Brush & Bevel had learned by bitter experience to hold off on ordering supplies for any of her framing pieces.

"Oh, good morning, Ginny," she called out. "Hello, Sue, I'm glad you're here today. Look what I've found!" She bustled up to the design table and began to unwrap a long narrow piece of art. "The frame is hideous, but I just fell in love with the image," she gushed as the paper fell away. "Don't you just love it?"

Sue could not meet Ginny's eyes. To tell the truth, the driftwood frame was the only worthwhile part of the piece. The two mats were inexpensive ones, the wrong colors entirely. They already showed the telltale stains of unbuffered acidity, terribly damaging to artwork. The picture, a cheap print of an amateur painting, made Sue want to shudder: a languorous curve of sandy tropical beach, a rocky breakwater straight out of Bar Harbor, Maine, palm trees from the Caribbean, and four oversized sailboats with hideous bright sails. The palms and the sails were blowing in different directions. Ginny was biting her lip.

"It's great, Sunny." Sue rubbed her nose with a forefinger. "Where did you find it?"

While the woman rattled on about "this marvelous little shop in Newburyport," Sue busied herself freeing the frame of its contents. It was an attractive bit of driftwood and never should have been asked to house the cheap, acidic mats already staining the paper of the print. Sue dropped the greasy, wavy glass into the trash and resigned herself to the fact that Sunny would want a cherry frame, even though cherry would clash with the improbable beach in the picture.

Sure enough, Sunny was already yanking cherry samples off the rug-covered wall, wrenching them as though they were epoxied rather than velcroed. She turned around just as Sue placed two new mats on top of the original discolored ones. "Oh. How interesting. I think I like that. What a difference they make!"

"If you'd like," Sue offered, "I can unmount the print so the old mats aren't so distracting. When we remount it, we'll use acid-free tape, of course."

"Do you always use acid-free tape?"

"We haven't used acid in years," Sue assured her. Ginny, who'd wandered off to answer the phone, choked to conceal her laughter at the double entendre.

An hour later, Sue sent Sunny out the door with a pile of mat samples and half a dozen frame corners, none of them cherry. She collapsed in one of the upholstered armchairs Ginny used to make customers feel at home. "I'm gonna kill her, Ginny," she moaned. "I swear I'll kill her. Right after I kill you for tossing her at me!"

Ginny laughed at Sue's theatrics. "What was she talking about with those darned beach stones?"

"She wanted them glued to the frame. At least I convinced her I couldn't dye them. Now she wants me to paint them to match the sails!" Sue rolled her eyes, then shut them and let her head fall back against the chair.

"We've got to think of something else." Ginny looked worried. "I can't let her get away with something like that. It'll look horrible."

"Can't look any worse than it already does," Sue murmured, her eyes still closed.

Ginny agreed. "Don't worry about it, Sue. You know she'll be back in a week with some other crazy idea."

Sue sighed and looked at the clock. "Looks like I'd better go get some work done, but I do want to hear more about Jerry Berger when you have time."

****

While Ginny and Sue dealt with Sunny, Elsie was enjoying the tentative warmth of an early spring day. Although snow still clung to the shady spots and ice rimmed the melt-swollen streams, the ground was thawing. Mud was everywhere.

A lot of the mud adhered to her young, brown and white bird dog, Maculato. *Stupid name for a dog. And why was a German short-haired pointer given the name "Spot" in Italian?* A puppy hadn't been her idea, but when her husband, Frank, had brought him home, she'd fallen in love with the wiggling little bundle of affection. Now she wouldn't trade him for the world.

Mac had a positive genius for finding the muddiest places along their regular walks. Today, he discovered the joys of chasing the hordes of frogs on their way to the breeding grounds in the vernal ponds. The first frog he sniffed alongside the road sat absolutely still until he'd sniffed just a little too long. The frog burst into motion, pushed off Mac's brown-spotted nose, and dove into the underbrush.

This was a marvelous game. The dog almost yanked Elsie's arm off when he sprang after the frog. She had a major tussle with him before he came to heel. Then there were other frogs to chase, all the way down to the bridge that was their turn-around point, and then all the way back home. Mac had found his calling; he was a frog dog.

Maybe I could rent him out to Jemmie to guard his storeroom.

She enjoyed a quiet laugh at the thought. Jemmie's obsession with "critters" was ridiculous. He was a prize-winning jeweler, but he just didn't seem to know how to get along with people. If it weren't for his staff buffering customers from his outbursts, his business would never survive. Just last week he'd harangued his employees loudly enough to be heard through the walls, and he swore a blue streak whenever the garage door was up longer than he thought it should be.

Elsie sighed. Except for Jemmie, working at Brush & Bevel was wonderful. Not even that unsettling incident with Mike Bingham could diminish her pleasure in the job, even though it had scared her at the time.

The new Jerry Berger only added to her job satisfaction. Elsie had no doubt it was his work. Didn't she deal with his art all the time? She even recognized Abby as the woman in the painting. She hoped Jenna would agree to deal with Ginny over the painting. She wanted to see it again, cleaned up, framed, and celebrated as it should be. It would be a fine memorial to a woman who didn't deserve to die.

Not that Jerry deserved to die, of course. Not for one minute had Elsie ever accepted the conclusion he died by his own hand. Jerry was no saint; his obsession with his art made living with him impossible. Elsie paused in her mud-cleaning; she had never before noticed a similarity between Jemmie Demarais and Jerry Berger. Jerry had pestered poor Abby until at last she agreed to sit for him, just to shut him up. He was demanding and self-centered, like so many artists who saw everything through the lens of their art. Still, he was bright and eager, full of life. He made people feel glad to be around him. The day he brought *A Walk in the Rain* to the shop for framing, he'd been so excited—bursting with well-justified pride, sure this was his breakthrough painting, the one that would make his career. He'd been right. It made his career. His career took off; he was successful and happy, Elsie was sure of that. He would never have killed himself, or anyone else. Why, she had seen him release insects that got through the screen downstairs.

Mike Bingham, now, he was another story. Elsie could picture him squashing bugs, pulling the wings off flies, or worse. She had seen murder in his eyes that day at the gallery, even in the dimness of the still-closed shop. He was a hard man, a ruthless politician in the big city of Mill Falls. Perhaps it was just as well he wouldn't let Abby adopt a child. No one could have grown up happy with such a man as a father.

Well, Jerry and Abby were dead. Mike was off being ruthless in some hapless city out in Arizona or California. Elsie had better things to do than think about the past.

Chapter Five

A week passed with no more word from Jenna
Rudolph. Ginny explained to her employees the fair
terms she had offered Jenna to display the little nude if
it was confirmed as a Berger. Jerry's brother Howard
and sister Pam were his heirs. She would give them the
first option to buy it if Jenna decided to sell, but Ginny
really wanted to have the piece in her gallery. She was
already mulling over plans for an unveiling and a big
advertising campaign.

She was sure there would be a market for prints of
the painting. Jerry still had a devoted following and
sales of his prints were steady, if not spectacular.
Obviously, she couldn't issue the usual signed and
numbered limited edition, since the artist was no longer
available to sign the prints. Other estates, however, had
offered limited editions, numbered and countersigned
by someone close to the artist—a spouse, a model, a
close relative. She did some quiet checking into those
possibilities while she awaited Jenna's decision.

In the meantime, business went on as usual at
Brush & Bevel. Sunny came back in and traded the
sample mats Sue had given her for others that would
"work better with my furniture" as she put it, even
though they were not right for the print of palms in Bar
Harbor. In a lighthearted moment, Sue and Elsie
assembled a large group of frog portraits, all displaying

their absolute and total lack of teeth, and pinned it to Jemmie's storeroom door. They could hear him screaming with alarm when he found it, and then they heard the denials of his employees.

"Maybe we should 'fess up," Sue suggested with a sheepish look on her face. "I didn't mean to scare him."

"Let him calm down first." Ginny had enjoyed the joke as much as her workers did. She had no patience with the man's quirks. "You told him frogs don't have teeth."

"Over and over. He doesn't believe me."

The screaming two doors over continued, and Mark Horner, the tall, thin owner and chef at The Chowdah Bowl, popped in to see if they knew what was going on. He brought a sample bowl of his latest recipe with him. He jerked his head toward the jeweler's. "If he doesn't shut up soon, I'm calling the cops."

At that moment, the noise stopped as if a plug had been pulled. Mark shrugged. "Try this." He offered the bowl. "Tell me what you think."

The three women each dipped a spoon into the soup and tasted. They chewed thoughtfully, swallowed, and looked at each other.

"Are you going to tell him?" Elsie asked Ginny.

"I thought you would." Ginny shook her head and turned to Sue with an expectant look.

"Not me! You're the boss."

Ginny sighed and looked into the bowl again. Mark tipped it considerately toward her, looking hopeful, but she declined. "Mark, I gotta tell you…I gotta say…" She wet her lips and started over. "Mark, that is absolutely the worst thing you've ever brought us. It's too salty, the potatoes are overdone, and I think the fish was past its sale date. I can't believe you made it."

Mark's mobile face fell as he looked at each of the women in turn. "You really think so? It's that bad?" They all agreed it was pretty bad chowder, not nearly good enough for The Chowdah Bowl.

"If you try to sell that, you'll kill the Bowl," Elsie said. She loved seafood, especially chowder.

As they nodded in dolorous agreement, he let out a sudden whoop. "I knew it! I knew they'd screw it up!" He burst into laughter, spreading his arms and shaking his head. "I didn't make it," he explained when he began to settle down. "My supplier is trying to sell me that stuff. He says it's his best seller, all the big restaurants use it!"

"Well, that explains it," Ginny remarked. "No wonder everyone comes to you, if that's the best they can get anywhere else." She started to say more, but nothing came out of her mouth as she stared out the window to the parking lot. "I don't believe it!"

They all turned to look. Jemmie's four assistants were marching out to their cars, jackets and purses slung over their shoulders. They realized someone was watching and waved cheerily. One of the women, Sandy, veered over to Brush & Bevel and poked her head in the door. "We've had it," she said, without much distress. "Jemmie's out of his mind, and we can't take any more of his abuse."

Sue made a face. "Look, I put those pictures up. Do you want me to apologize?"

Sandy chuckled. "No, no. I'm glad you did. We've put up with so much of his nonsense, and that was the final straw. It just all added up and here we are."

"But—your jobs," Ginny protested.

"Oh, we'll be back tomorrow. It's just that we told Jemmie we would walk out the next time he started in on us, and we did it. If he starts up again, we'll walk out again. Sooner or later, he'll catch on. Bye!"

Mark slapped his knee as he watched her go. "The man needs more than a walkout, but it's a start! Hey, next time can we call the cops?"

In the end, as they all headed back to work, they decided to leave it up to Jemmie's employees, unless he started in on someone else.

The tracking board was pleasantly full with plenty of frame orders to work on. Sue asked Elsie to check a measurement before she ordered a frame, then they worked together to assemble an oversized print.

Ginny turned back to her paperwork, but the altercation at Jemmie's upset her. If he could get so upset over frog pictures, what might he do if something serious happened? What could she do about it? She put in a call to the Westford police and asked to have an officer stop by for a consultation.

****

Two days later, just after nine o'clock, Officer Tom DiAndreo pulled up in front of Brush & Bevel and knocked on the locked door. Ginny let him in and offered coffee.

"Only if you're having some," he replied. "Unfortunately, some folks would consider it an 'inducement.'"

Ginny rolled her eyes. "I'll get some for both of us. Sue and Elsie already have theirs." When she returned with the cups, he was staring upward. She followed his gaze but couldn't determine what he was looking at.

She nudged his elbow. "Something interesting up there?"

He grinned boyishly and accepted the coffee. "Nice ceiling. No spitballs."

"I should hope not." She raised an eyebrow, inviting an explanation.

"There are sixteen spitballs in the ceiling over my desk. Been there since I started twelve years ago. I keep complaining, but the cleaning staff never gets rid of 'em."

Ginny chuckled. "That's why I do my own cleaning."

"Yeah, well, the town won't spend money on a decent cleaning service. They'd rather spend it on 'essentials' like fireworks." He shook his head and took a swig of coffee. "This is good. Thanks. Gets the dust of the file room out of my throat."

"Let me guess, they won't spring for a proper filing system, either."

He winked. "One reason I'm applying to the state police."

Within a few minutes, Ed the landlord showed up and Carol from the deli came in, too. They each took a seat, some in the upholstered chairs and some on the tall swivel chairs.

Mark scooted in and perched a hip on the design desk. DiAndreo stood beside the faux fireplace and waited until the chitchat died down.

"You don't look very surprised to see us all," Ginny said.

"Let me guess. It's about Jemmie Demarais, right?"

At their nod, he sighed. "Any time you feel

threatened, I mean *any* time, call us. We'll be right over. We all know he's got a couple screws loose, even though we don't think he'd actually hurt anyone. He doesn't have to hurt someone to get in trouble with the law. Just threatening can be a crime. Now, do you have anything concrete against him?"

They looked at each other, but it was Ginny who jumped in first. "He's a royal pain, although I've never been afraid of him. I think he needs help, but I'm certainly not going to say that to him."

"No, I don't think you should. It has to come from somebody close to him, or else from an official. Leave that part of it alone. What about his staff?"

"They yell back, and now they've started walking out," Elsie said. "I don't want another situation like the one ten years ago…" She paused to see if DiAndreo remembered when Mike Bingham had frightened her so and went on at his nod, "and it's not right that our customers have to hear that kind of stuff."

"Does he get profane? Because if he does, we can charge him with indecency."

"Not that I've heard," Ginny started, but Mark spoke over her.

"He's got a potty mouth and he's loud, but he doesn't threaten. He's just so weird!"

Carol, who had been quiet up 'til now, said, "I've heard things out of him I wouldn't want my kids to hear. He scares some of the high schoolers who work for me in the afternoons. One girl even quit because of him."

The policeman said, "I think I have enough information here that I'd be justified in having a talk with him. Do you want me to?"

Since it had come to decision time, everyone paused for a deep breath. Ed the landlord was the first to break the silence. "I would appreciate it, Tom. I don't expect my tenants to be one big happy family, but when you've got one that upsets everyone else, it can be a big problem. I don't have quite enough to kick him out, but sometimes I'd like to."

Ginny summed it up. "In the end, it's up to you, Tom."

DiAndreo looked around the room. "Okay. I'll stop in over the next couple of days sometime. I don't want it to look like I've come directly from all of you guys. Does that work?"

There were murmured thanks and a general sense of relief. After Tom DiAndreo got back into his cruiser, everyone talked for a few minutes before returning to their respective shops.

Mark Horner thanked Ginny for arranging the meeting, and said with complete sincerity, "You know you gals can always call any of us at the Bowl any time you need us. I'm serious. We'll come right over and jump on him if we have to."

The thought sparked one of Elsie's silly moods. "I can see it now," she giggled. "One outraged gorilla—that's Jemmie—two little froggies, and half a bushel of quahogs. And me and Sue with shards of glass in our hands!"

They laughed. "Who needs glass?" Sue said. "We have razor blades, X-Acto knives, box cutters. Even fallouts from beveled mats are sharp enough to cut skin."

"Not to mention my kitchen," Mark added. "Chopping blades, paring knives, and a meat slicer could do lots of damage."

Ginny nodded. If someone wanted to do harm, there were plenty of deadly weapons to choose from, ready to hand. She shivered.

Chapter Six

April turned to May; the daily routine of Brush & Bevel was busy enough to prevent Ginny, Sue, and Elsie from spending too much energy on any one problem. The Berger painting—though never forgotten—faded into the background behind the Jemmie incident and the wedding rush. Every year, it seemed, it became more popular to have a photo of the happy couple displayed at the reception in lieu of a guest book, with an extra-wide mat for guests to pen their best wishes and sign their names. Brush & Bevel now stocked an assortment of precut mats and ready-made frames for the convenience of harried brides, or more likely maids of honor or mothers of the bride, who never seemed to remember the memento until the last moment.

Besides the routine framing, there were always the unusual objects customers wanted to preserve. May often meant souvenirs of First Communions, christenings, and gifts for teachers. This year a dance school wanted to honor a retiring teacher by framing a pair of her ballet slippers, and an equestrienne brought in a bronzed set of her horse's shoes. The staff always enjoyed the creative challenge such items entailed.

Sunny returned one day to finalize her mat choice. She also brought along a handful of stones that had been fitted with snug coats of felt in swirls of bright colors. Her idea was to set them in the frame as if they were part of the beach. Ginny, her lips twitching, dissuaded her by pointing out the stones were way out of proportion. "Well, can you paint the frame? In swirls like the felt?" the irrepressible woman asked.

Ginny hid her amusement as best she could and thanked the stars Sue was downstairs at the moment. "We could, Sunny, but you're artistic. Why don't you do it? Then it would be exactly what you want."

The red-dyed hair bobbed as Sunny nodded. "Do you really think I could?"

"Of course," Ginny assured her and rubbed her nose. Sunny danced out the door on clouds of elation.

A week after Sunny's visit, in mid-May, Jenna Rudolph returned at last to Brush & Bevel with the painting they all believed was a Jerry Berger. Her round, pleasant face was quite serious as she entered. Sue and Elsie started to excuse themselves, to allow Ginny to complete the agreement in private, but Jenna asked them to stay. "You should hear this. You will be caring for this painting, and I want you to know how I feel."

Ginny settled them all in the "living room" area of the shop, where the upholstered chairs and a faux fireplace created a cozy nook. She offered coffee or a soda from the deli, but Jenna declined. It was a Tuesday, usually a rather slow day when few customers came in and the staff could count on getting a lot of framing done. "I'm glad you decided to go ahead," Ginny began.

Jenna shrugged. "Well, I sort of feel I have to. I almost feel like I owe it to this painting." She held it up on her lap, studying it for a moment. "I didn't like it at first. I've never been very fond of nudes. And to think of a woman naked in the woods like this, and an artist sitting there doing her portrait—well, it makes me rather uncomfortable."

"If it's any consolation," Ginny interjected, "Jerry—if this really is his, which I think it is—Jerry usually worked from photographs. He would have taken pictures of the rocks, maybe when she was with him, maybe not. If she was there, she was probably clothed. Then he would have photographed her in his studio and combined the two. I don't think he would have made her sit for hours out in the woods."

Jenna considered that, nodded, and continued. "The more I looked at it, the more I came to like it. It isn't—naughty, you know. She's quite pretty really. Then when I heard about how she died…I did some research and looked at his other paintings. I like them. I read about how he killed her and then himself, and I wondered why he would have done it. Then I thought, maybe she deserves to have her side of the story told." She ran her fingers along the edge of the canvas and laid the painting on her lap. "I've just about decided to go ahead, but I want to know as much as possible about it. About her and the artist, I mean. About how they died. What can you tell me?"

Ginny settled deeper into her chair. She had half-expected this request for more information. People were endless gossips, and a murder was juicy enough without adding in the suicide bit. She cast back in her mind. "It was a long time ago, the year we had so many big snowstorms early in the winter, everyone thought we'd be buried until Easter. The first I heard of it was when the newspapers reported Abby Bingham missing. I couldn't believe it. She was such a nice lady. Always doing things for the community. Anyway, it was right after a really big storm, and at first, the police thought she'd gotten into some kind of accident in the snow. So they were checking all the hospitals and so on. Then they thought maybe she and her husband Mike had been fighting and she ran away, but that turned out to be a dead end. The story faded away for a while, a couple of weeks at least. You know how it is: new stories get the front-page coverage, and it was right before Christmas. Mike kept bugging the cops, I heard."

Elsie stirred, but kept quiet. Mike had done a lot more than bug the cops, but Ginny wanted to stick with a sanitized version of the story.

"Then, I think it was the day after Christmas, or maybe it was right after New Year's, a couple of hunters were out in a field up north of here, tracking some deer, and they practically fell over the bodies. There had been a light snow, so they were covered, but it was obvious they were dead. They had, um…been there a long time, long enough for the coyotes to get at them." Ginny swallowed hard. "The hunters called the cops right away. The cops came and got what they could, and eventually figured out it was Jerry and Abby. From what they could piece together," she grimaced at her choice of words, "he shot her and then himself. But I never understood it. I never would've pictured him with a gun."

Jenna nodded. "But it's so mysterious, what people do. It could have been a murder/suicide. The cops thought it was." It sounded as though she was trying to convince herself. Her fingers tightened on the painting again. Her voice grew firmer. "All the more reason to put it out there. It's a terrible story, but people should hear it!"

"I'd go softly on that point," Ginny cautioned. "The police did decide it was murder/suicide, but the case is still open. I don't want to do anything that would damage their reputations or cause a scandal. The painting is good enough, or it should be once it's cleaned up, to add to Jerry's status, and that's all I care about. If we go forward with this, Jenna, I want you to understand that. This is about the art, that's all. Even though you own the painting itself, Jerry's family would be very upset if we raked up that old dirt about his death. I'm afraid I have to be firm about that."

After a long moment, Jenna inclined her head. "Well, let's just start by confirming this is really a Jerry Berger. Can we go over the agreement again?"

****

Sue and Elsie excused themselves, choking down their curiosity. Ginny would never reveal the contents of the agreement, of course. She was adamant about protecting the privacy of her clients. There were certain details they would have to know, such as whether and how the piece would be framed, and what the asking price would be if Jenna decided to sell it; maybe even the lowest price Jenna would accept, though that was something a potential buyer would never know. But sooner or later, they were sure, she would tell them why she had held back so much of the story from Jenna.

Sue offered to join frames today, but Elsie urged her to do the mat cutting instead. As a rule they shared all the various duties involved in completing the orders, but there was no sense denying they each had particular skills. Elsie had a real knack for getting sometimes-recalcitrant frame legs to join together without gaps, and Sue knew her way around the computer better than Elsie did. Both of them knew how to pin needlework and prepare works for dry mounting, but Sue enjoyed pinning while Elsie didn't, and the aerosol adhesive used to dry-mount less valuable prints didn't make Elsie sick as it did to Sue.

"I do need to get some practice on the computer," Elsie said, "but you know how long it takes me to do a mat. Yaneque will be here before lunch to pick up those mats to take to Keene."

"Oh, geez!" Sue exclaimed. "I forgot about them. I'd better get a move on!"

She booted up the computer and turned on the compressor for the cutter. While they warmed up, she gathered the mats she needed to cut and the four relevant work orders with the specifications. The mat cutters in general were very versatile, but the one at a gallery in Keene was an older model that couldn't handle the required cuts. The Keene gallery had called and asked Brush & Bevel to cut them; they'd faxed the designs and arranged for a pickup.

Sue looked over the first design, a complex one with multiple openings, a triple mat, and several decorative flourishes. She would have to keep her mind on business when she would rather be thinking about the Berger painting.

After nearly an hour of painstaking work, she was satisfied with the project. She cut the remaining three designs and wrapped them for Yaneque to pick up and take to Keene.

****

Elsie, meanwhile, set up the joiner and eight frames. For a wonder, they all went together so well she only had to set one frame into the vices for additional gluing. She was relieved. She wanted to think about her memories of Jerry and Abby while she worked.

What was Ginny holding back, and why? Did she have reservations about the police conclusion that it was murder/suicide? She wondered if Ginny had more information.

It had seemed so inexplicable back when it happened. There was no tension that anyone knew of between Abby and Jerry, or between Abby and Mike. Jerry lived alone, but he was at ease with both men and women. Elise smiled to herself, remembering how much she'd enjoyed it when Jerry came into the gallery. She had liked Abby, too, without complication. They were both nice people.

So who might have killed them? The police had cleared Mike Bingham, and judging by his demeanor, he'd been devastated by Abby's death. Elsie could never think back to that day when he appeared in the gallery without a shudder. Even now, her heart leaped into her throat sometimes when she opened the stairwell door. It was uncanny how he'd sat in the dark, gun in his lap, waiting. Just waiting. He perched on one of the tall chairs at the design table, and when she came through the door, he turned and snarled at her. It was almost an animal sound, deep in the throat, and that sound alone was enough to root her to the spot. Glaring straight at Elsie, he had demanded to know where he could find Abby.

Of course she'd had no answer. She said something inane, something about how the police were still looking for her. It was only then she saw the gun. A handgun, and though she had no idea what brand or caliber it was, it looked very lethal. Mike held his hand over it, not gripping it, thank God. That was all that saved him from a jail sentence; he hadn't made an actual threat with the gun.

Ginny filed charges, of course. As sympathetic as anyone could be toward a man almost insane with grief, she still refused to let him get away with invading her business and frightening her employees. He paid a fine, surrendered the gun, and agreed to attend some anger management sessions. Elsie couldn't remember whether he'd finished them.

After Abby's funeral and his court appearance to settle the trespass charges, Mike went away. He couldn't bear to live in Mill Falls anymore, he announced when he resigned his position as alderman. No one blamed him much. He went someplace out west, to a dry flat country as different as possible from the tree-covered mountains of New Hampshire. Over time most folks forgot about him.

Now it had all come back to haunt them. Why were memories of sudden death so vivid? How could such a minimal connection with the victims have become such a scar on their hearts? Brush & Bevel's owner had had only a business relationship with the Binghams, and not much more with Berger, however much she admired him. Elsie realized then that she couldn't remember just how Ginny had become involved with Berger's estate; she would have to ask her boss to refresh her memory.

Chapter Seven

Just after noon, Yaneque Duprey glided in the back door, calling out a cheerful hello to announce her presence. Elsie liked the courier. She was tall and slightly built, graceful yet efficient in her movements. Her coffee-brown skin glowed with confidence, and she wore her hair in elaborate cornrows that trailed off into long, thin braids. Today the braids were caught up into an elegant knot and held in place with a brightly-colored clip at the back of her head.

"Hi, Yaneque," Elsie greeted her. "Sue is just getting the mats bagged up for you. How are things with you? Business good?"

"Fine, thanks. When I got the second car and hired a helper a couple of years ago, I wasn't sure I'd have enough work for us both, but we're busy all the time. I'm starting to think of getting a third car and driver, but we're not quite there yet." She smiled, revealing even white teeth with a gap between the incisors. She had confided once that her dentist wanted to put braces on her teeth, to close up the gap. Yaneque had been adamant she wouldn't do it; an old African tradition held that such a gap was a "god-hole," a mark of special favor, and some believed those who were blessed with one had special powers. "Like the people who have 'the Sight'?" Ginny had asked. "Something like that," Yaneque had replied, without explaining any further.

"Would you have to give up driving, if you had that many cars on the road?" Elsie asked.

"Sometimes I think I should give it up now. The paperwork takes so much time!" Yaneque answered. "I'd hate to, though. I like being out and about."

"Even in the winter?" Elsie hated winter driving and couldn't imagine anyone enjoying it. She reddened, embarrassed at referring to that long-ago accident. "I'm sorry, didn't mean to bring that up."

Yaneque was not offended. "Even in the winter. I like a challenge. Since I don't remember anything about the accident, it's never bothered me much."

"Really?" Sue walked in from the joining room, toting the package of mats. "I knew someone who had meningitis once. She collapsed at a firehouse picnic and forgot most of the next month. But eventually she got back most of those memories. She never remembered collapsing, though, and she never liked going back to the firehouse, even though she had no memory of getting sick there."

Yaneque shook her head. "Nope, I don't even have that. I go over Temple Mountain all the time and it doesn't bother me at all. I just have this feeling there was something I didn't get done. Which makes sense, in a way, because I do remember that when I left home that day I had two errands to run. Later on, after I got out of the hospital, I figured out one of them, because the client called me to wish me well. He reminded me I canceled his errand that day. But I've never figured out what the other one was."

Yaneque looked over the packaging of the mats to be sure it was secure. Sue had placed the mats between two sheets of corrugated cardboard, taped them together, and wrapped it all in a clear plastic bag, which she sealed with packing tape. One of the advantages of using RunAround, besides the quick delivery time, was the less intense packing that had to be done. Parcels were picked up and delivered with a minimum of handling.

Yaneque gave a sharp nod. "Looks good. I'll have it out there in a few hours."

Sue stuck her fingers in her jeans pocket, a sure sign she was getting ready to chat. "I've been wondering. Other than that big accident, have you ever had any serious trouble with your business?"

"A few fender-benders and a couple of speeding tickets, that's all, knock on wood. I make enough to live on."

Just then the upstairs doorbell rang. Elsie listened a moment to see if it was Jenna leaving or another customer entering, in which case Ginny would need help.

Apparently, Jenna had left, because the stairwell door opened and they recognized the boss's footsteps on the stairs. Yaneque paused on her way out the door to say hello.

Carrying the alleged Berger painting before her like the Holy Grail, Ginny marched in, a surprisingly sad look on her face. She gave Yaneque a warm greeting and then laid the painting on the worktable.

"What a nice picture!" the delivery woman exclaimed.

They all turned their eyes to it. It sat on the table, mute, as if it waited for something. Ginny glanced at Yaneque, then looked away.

"Are you going to frame it?" Yaneque asked.

"I think so," Ginny answered. "First, we'll be cleaning it up a bit. It's been gathering grease in a bar for ten years." Again she glanced at Yaneque.

She took the hint. "Well, I'd better be on my way. Have a good day!" And she strode out to the brightly-painted car parked behind the building.

Ginny sighed.

"Did you get the contract all worked out?" Elsie asked.

"What? Oh, yes, we did." Ginny seemed to come out of some inner dialogue. "We're going to clean it up—can you do that soon, Sue? It doesn't have to be right away, but sometime in the next week would be good. After that, we'll see. I think Jenna wants to keep it, and she has every right. But if it really is a Berger, it would be a shame to hang it over her fireplace where no one else can appreciate it."

"Do you think—always assuming it is what we think it is—it would be very valuable?" Elsie asked.

"Of course, you can never tell," Ginny temporized, "but there have been some feelers about one of his other originals. I can't say anything yet, and don't you even hint about this, but it would be an important sale. I won't even tell you which one!" she added, recognizing the glint in their eyes. "And this one, being an unknown…"

"I'll get it cleaned as soon as I can," Sue promised. "I want to know if there really is a signature under there."

"What I want to know," Elsie murmured, "is how it got from Jerry's studio to a bar on the Cape."

Sue turned the painting over to look at the mounting and the strainers. "It really should be taken off these moldy strips and remounted. What did Jenna say about that?"

"She won't do anything until after it's been cleaned. If it is a Berger, then we'll talk again."

Chapter Eight

Ginny Brent decided she would do the next step in her investigation from her home near the seacoast rather than at the gallery. She didn't want to have a customer walk in while she was on the phone with this chore. So the next day, after she had her stroll on the beach—the warmth of spring still lay in the future, but the sea air was so refreshing—she sat at the desk in her home office with a scotch on the rocks and the name Jenna Rudolph had provided.

One of the problems with identifying a previously unknown painting was its "provenance," or what the police would call the chain of custody. Even if a recognized authority, in this case Ginny herself, was certain a work belonged to a particular artist, and even if the brushwork and signature withstood the scrutiny of knowledgeable experts, it was still best to know how the work got from the artist's studio to its present location. Ginny had one end of the thread—the painting of the nude. The other end was Jerry Berger's studio in Douglass. In between, an unknown tangle of threads would—or would not—connect the ends.

She prepared her story with care. She couldn't blurt out she'd come across a painting that might be valuable, or she'd have rumors flying and former owners trying to claim it. It seemed obvious Bob Rudolph had bought the painting at a legitimate auction, and therefore, he had the legal rights. Beyond that, things got a little knotty.

The first step was to contact the auction house. Fortunately, Jenna had found the receipt for the purchase, dated two months earlier. Ginny tapped in the telephone number of North Shore Sales and waited.

The phone rang for a long time. No answering machine picked up, and she let it ring. Eight rings, nine, ten.

"No'th Shaw Sales," said a male voice with a strong Cape Cod accent. "Mitch."

"Mitch," she began, making her voice warm and feminine, "I'm trying to track down an item that was sold at your sale about two months ago. How do I go about it?"

"Hey, once it's sold we got nothin' more to do with it." Mitch was cautious and impatient. "It's gone and outta heah."

"No, I'm going the other way. I'm trying to find out where it came from and see if I can get another one. There would be a commission for your help." She sweetened her voice to tempt him.

He paused and she heard a grating noise in the phone. She pictured him scratching an unshaven chin. "Whatcha got?"

"It's a painting, about sixteen by twenty. It was in a sale of items from a bar that went out of business. Do you remember that?"

"I'd have to look it up, and it's busy around heah."

"Is there someone else who would have the time to talk to me?"

More scratching. Evidently, the idea of a commission intrigued Mitch, and he reconsidered his hurry. "Bahs're always goin' outta business. What's it look like?"

Ginny described it. "It's in the woods, some big rocks, and a nude woman in the rocks, looking over her shoulder. She's sort of leaning on one of the rocks, pointing toward something or other."

"Lemme think." Grunts and hums came through the phone, along with the sound of papers being rustled. "Yeah. I wasn't heah when it sold. I saw it, though. Was it the chick with the big a—" he corrected himself. "The big rear?"

Ginny choked down her laugh. "That's it."

"Well, hell, yeah. We all liked that one, kinda surprised it didn't disappeah before it got to the block, y'know what I mean?" He chuckled, coughing as if he realized it might not be a good idea to reveal so much, and continued. "Anyway, says heah it went for a good price. I can't give ya the name of the buyah, y'know."

She hastened to agree. "Of course not. I'm looking for the name of the artist, or if you don't have that, the name of the bar owner."

His suspicion returned. "What good would that do ya?"

"Maybe he knows the name of the artist. See, a friend bought the painting. My husband likes it so much I thought I'd try to get another one by the same guy. For a birthday present." She touched her fingers to her nose and stretched her arm out. She'd outdo Pinocchio yet. Nosy gal, indeed!

More papers rustled. "Well, that's a little sticky, too. What I can do for ya is, I can give him *your* number, and he can call *you* if he wants. That do ya?"

Ginny hesitated. The last thing she wanted was to

have some retired barkeeper calling her. But that was a prejudice; she would think of him as a reasonable businessman, and she knew how to speak that language. She gave Mitch her number, and added, "Please tell him my husband's birthday is coming up next month, so I'd appreciate it if he could get back to me before then. Better yet, can I send you a note for him, Mitch? That way you'll have it all written down for him."

"Yuh, that'll do. You send it to me, and I'll take care of it for ya." He repeated his address twice, without quite saying he expected a tip in the note.

Ginny thanked him and was glad to hang up. Dealing with people like that made her feel dirty. Not that there was anything wrong with offering a "consideration." Mitch had taken time out of his busy day, and otherwise had no incentive to help her. A favor was a favor, after all. She debated for a while before she decided on how much cash to send—a little now, and a little more when and if the barkeeper called.

Her chair squeaked as she leaned back and took a pull on the scotch. She welcomed the shock of it going down her throat, a counterirritant to her regrets. Seeing Abby Bingham in that painting, knowing Jerry had painted her in the nude, felt like a rasp drawn across her skin. It wasn't love, never love, that bound Ginny to the artist. Lust, maybe, on both sides. For her, Jerry had been a reawakening of longings she'd thought herself long past. She could tell herself it was his art, his dedication to his work that drew her to him. She could, sometimes, convince herself she was the teacher who came along when Jerry, the student, was ready. She guided him, molded him, showed him how to be a better artist; she taught him how to market himself as

56

well as his art. That was the proper role for an older woman like her, and she played it well. But somehow, when she thought of Jerry Berger, it wasn't the way his sales improved under her tutelage or the expanding power of his vision that she remembered.

She closed her eyes, but she couldn't block out the memories. Behind her eyelids, it was Jerry's vivid blue eyes she remembered, and the way they blazed with the force of the creative vision she helped him bring to life. It was those magical afternoons in his studio, redolent of oil paint and turpentine, when he would dip a supple brush in a thin wash of color and run it down her arm or feather it across the fine hairs on the back of her neck. "Are you going to paint me?" she'd asked, and he hadn't said a word, merely replacing the brush with his lips.

There was something incredibly alluring in the utter security of knowing they would hear anyone approach on the gravel road long before they could be observed, and something ritualistic about the careful way Jerry would cover his canvas and shut off the phone before he took her hand and led her upstairs.

A slow tear trickled down her cheek. *Dammit, it's over. It was over when he moved to that big-time printer, before he ever met Abby. And dammit, he met Abby in my shop! And me, stupid generous me, I urged her to work with him.*

How could I have been so dumb?

The anger drained away, replaced by a cold, dragging misery. Here she was, a woman whose marriage hadn't survived her affair, crying over a man ten years dead. Abby was dead, too. Seeing her portrait made Ginny remember how much she'd liked the younger woman. Maybe she even realized Abby was much better for Jerry than she could ever have been. A bitter thought.

Her glass had gotten empty somehow. It was too much work to go refill it. She put her head down on the desk and wept.

Chapter Nine

"My turn," Sue said to Elsie when the doorbell rang a few days later. She was glad to take a break from her current task of preparing Sunny's frame. "I swear I don't need the gym with all this running up and down the steps!"

She trotted up and paused at the top to catch her breath. When she opened the door, the Costas, two of her very favorite customers, were waiting for her. "Hello!" she called out with a broad smile. "Walt and Linda, how are you?"

Warm smiles returned her greeting. They were a curious couple. Dressed in several layers of mismatched clothing, they leaned on each other like the two halves of an archway. Sue couldn't imagine them apart from each other. Perhaps, over the long years of their marriage, they had grown so intertwined that one could not stand without the other.

Certainly, Linda could barely stand without Walt. Some cruel blow, a stroke perhaps, had twisted her body until her right ear touched her shoulder and her shoulder nearly touched her hip. She looked sideways at the world through eyes that paradoxically shone with intelligence and good humor. Whatever damage had been done to her body had spared her mind; she was quick and more alert than many people far younger than her eighty-odd years.

Walt, on the other hand, stood straight as a flagpole, though his hands had a constant tremor. He carried Linda's voluminous purse across his chest like a bandolier, and often enough, he carried her cane as well. He doted on her as if she were the most precious thing in the world. And probably, Sue decided, she was. His arm curled around her like a bird's wing.

"What can I do for you lovely folks today?" she said.

"We came to see our trees," Linda teased.

"Well, come on, they're right over here in the corner, where they can get a little bit of sun." Sue led the way. An oversized planter held a pair of potted palms that had once belonged to the Costas. When they'd moved out of their big old farmhouse and into a condo, they put a large assortment of plants out for the neighbors to adopt. Elsie, arriving late at their house, had picked up the last planter, with the sorry-looking palms dropping their last leaves in her car. Not knowing what else to do with it, she brought it in to the gallery to fill an empty corner.

The palms thrived in their new home. They'd responded to a little pruning, some fortified soil, and a bit of judicious fertilizing by growing fresh leaves and adding several inches in height. Twice a week, the staff supplied them with water and gave the planter a quarter turn to keep them upright. Elsie even talked to them, calling them by the names of their former owners.

Sue moved aside one of the armchairs and pulled the planter on its casters out from the wall. "And look what they've been up to! Walt and Linda are having babies!"

"Oh, at our age!" Linda giggled like a schoolgirl.

"I told you we still have the right stuff." Walt puffed out his chest and grinned down at his life partner. He helped her to a seat and then, with grave dignity, accepted the other armchair.

"So, what can I do for you today?" Sue pulled over a wooden chair and sat down to face them.

"Well, our nephew's son is getting married," Linda began.

"Which one is he?" Though she could never sort out the Costas' many relatives, she knew they liked to talk about them. They seemed to be related to most everyone in town. Those who weren't relations they knew well.

"To tell the truth, he's more like a grandson. Our daughter Angela raised him after that awful car crash when he was young, so he grew up with our grandchildren Shelley and Tony. He's a policeman, you know."

"Tony's a policeman? I thought he was a dentist." Sue was confused at this spate of information.

"Yes, Tony's a dentist," Linda explained patiently. "Tommy is the one who is a policeman. Anyway, he's getting married, and we wanted to get him something for their new apartment. What do you suggest?"

"How about the wedding photo? You know, the kind people are doing now, with the big wide border for people to sign. That's very popular. All you need is a nice picture of the couple."

"What's wrong with a good old-fashioned guest book?" Linda objected. Walt nodded in agreement. "What else do you have?"

"Well, let me think. We have some nice romantic prints here that the artist will personalize for them, if you like any of them." Sue showed them half a dozen choices of relatively small prints, ranging from cute to classic, that were popular wedding gifts.

"Do they come framed?" Walt asked.

"No, they don't. You could frame it for them, but many people give a gift certificate for the framing, if they live near us. That way they can choose what they like."

The old couple consulted each other's eyes and came to a decision without speaking. "Okay, we'll take the one with the rose," Walt said. "What will the framing cost?"

Sue mentioned a price range, and Linda promptly chose the high end of it. Just by looking at them, no one could guess they were extremely well off. "Let them get something really nice. You'll help them, won't you, Sue?"

"Of course. Don't worry, we'll take good care of them. Now, what names do you want on the print?"

"Tom and Donna."

Sue took her time writing out the order, checking the spelling even on the simple names. Then she made up a gift certificate for the specified amount. "Do you want me to fill it in for you?"

"Yes, please," Linda said. "Make it to Mr. and Mrs. Thomas DiAndreo."

Sue did so, and then she exclaimed, "Oh! You mean Tom DiAndreo is your grandson? I know him! He's a cop here in town."

The Costas beamed at being able to surprise her. "You mean you didn't know that?"

"I know Tom, I didn't realize he was your grandson. Your nephew's son, I mean. I didn't know he was related to you."

"Well, now you do."

"He's a good cop," Sue added, mindful of his help with Jemmie.

Walt confided, "He wants to be a detective for the state police. So if you have any crimes that need solving…"

Sue grinned. "If I do, I'll be sure to call him. Please give him my congratulations, would you? And we'll call you as soon as the print comes in. It should be here by the end of next week."

She helped Walt assist Linda to the car, chatting to make it seem as though she was prolonging the visit rather than providing an arm to lean on. He tucked his wife into her seat, made sure her seatbelt didn't pinch, and with a wry chuckle let Sue slip her hand under his elbow. "I see you, young lady!" Linda sang out. "Don't you go stealing my man!"

"He's worth stealing," Sue shot back. "But I don't think I stand a chance against you."

Walt cackled, an old man's laugh full of good humor. "Either she won't let me out of her sight, or I'm too infatuated to look at anyone else," he said. But his eyes were soft and deep with worry and devotion. Sue watched him drive away and discovered her own eyes were moist. The courage of those two as they faced the end of their lives never failed to move her. Though Sue loved them, she could never see them without a pang of loss for her beloved Peter.

She went back inside, placed the order on Ginny's desk, and returned to the job she had so eagerly abandoned half an hour earlier. An assortment of aquarium gravel sat in plastic bags on the worktable downstairs. While she was working with the Costas, Elsie had cut the mats Sunny had finally decided on and mounted the print as well. It lay next to the bags of bright-colored gravel, along with a tub of tile grout.

"Thanks, Elsie," Sue began. "I guess I have to get on with it, don't I?"

"I'll do it, if you want," Elsie offered without any enthusiasm whatsoever.

Sue would have loved to accept the offer, but Sunny had asked specifically for her to do it. Where had Sunny come up with the zany idea to glue colored bits of stone to the driftwood frame? Well, at least Sunny had given up demanding she paint or dye the beach stones. Now she just wanted them nestled amid the gravel.

Sue sighed before she dug into the grout and applied it to the frame. The driftwood was the only good part of the package, and now it would be covered with neon shades of stone chips. Well, the customer was always right. Wasn't she?

An hour and a half later, she straightened her stiff back and studied her creation. Elsie cast dubious eyes at it, too. The two friends burst into laughter. "It's not really that bad, is it, Elsie?" Sue pleaded.

Elsie shook her head. "No. It's worse. But that's Sunny. She'll love it."

"What do you think? Should we make up a bunch of these to sell? I bet the world is just crying out for frames like this. Don't you think they'd fly out of here?"

"Oh, sure. On the business end of Ginny's broom!"

When they had finished their chuckle over that idea, they stored the embellished frame on a metal shelf to protect it from accidental bumps. By then it was time to close up the shop, so they put away their tools, shut down the computerized mat cutter, and turned off the air compressors before locking up.

"Have fun with the dog tomorrow," Sue said as they got into their cars.

Chapter Ten

Maculato needed a serious workout, Elsie decided. The dog was just beginning his second year, and after having been cooped up all winter, he was so giddy at getting outside into the lovely spring weather that he couldn't decide whether to chase his tail or hightail it into the woods. To tell the truth, Elsie was just as glad to have an excuse to get out of the house on her day off. She called an acquaintance to ask for permission to train the dog on his land. The permission duly given, she sprayed herself and Mac against the ubiquitous bugs, put him into the truck, and drove west toward Temple Mountain.

Just before the top of the pass, she took a right turn and headed north along a winding road bordered by thick woods, which were broken only by the occasional house. Most of them were new construction, with wide lawns and curving, paved driveways carved out of the forest. These houses had no actual residents; the owners were away from dawn to dusk at their jobs in Boston or Worcester. Sometimes they even lived in New York City from Sunday night to Friday evening, returning to spend the weekend in their oversized, overpriced mansions. Elsie much preferred the cramped old house she shared with Frank, despite its problematic wiring and its century of history, to these new-fangled bloats of modernity.

Never mind that. She counted three driveways beyond the amazingly pink house with the three-car garage, and then watched for the break in the stone wall on the left side of the road. She pulled into it, careful to angle the truck so its sides didn't scrape on the granite boulders some farmer had pulled out of the soil a hundred or more years ago. The young trees encroaching on the old wagon ruts showed that this had been pasture for cows or sheep as little as twenty-five years ago. Mac whined and pressed against the cage door as Elsie shut off the engine and came around to the back to snap on his leash.

A sudden silence fell as he leaped to the ground and began to snuffle around. Birds that had been advertising their availability flitted away. Elsie wanted to get Mac farther from the road before she released him, in order to keep distractions to a minimum and to prevent an accident. "Mac, come," she ordered. He sniffed a promising pile of debris one more time before turning to follow her up the wagon track.

The ruts led uphill, away from a small stream that gushed over rocks and exposed roots. Mac strained at the lead and got himself tangled in brush and branches every couple of minutes. After a ten-minute walk, they scrambled over another stone wall and into an abandoned apple orchard. This part of New Hampshire was rife with them, remnants of a once-thriving industry that eventually died because of the famous Yankee independence: where Washington State apple-growers banded together to promote their crop, stubborn New Englanders tried to go it alone. As a result, they lost out on volume discounts from the manufacturers of the necessary pesticides, and they lost out in terms of the power that comes from the united voices of many growers. They couldn't or wouldn't band together for their own good, so most of them went under. Literally under, in many cases—what had been orchard was often turned into housing lots, with names like "Orchard Row" or "Appletree Estates."

On this land, however, the orchard had just been allowed to fall into ruin. Grapes and brambles dragged some of the old trees into hummocks of green, providing shelter for birds and small mammals. Others, their once-pruned limbs thick with water-sprouts, stood lost among a riot of descendants. Deer had created paths that meandered among the trees. Elsie had to admonish Mac when he wanted to roll in their droppings. After a while, she came across the narrow lane the landowner mowed several times a year and followed it across a hay meadow and down into a wood.

Here at last she let Mac off the leash, holding his muzzle in her hand while she gave him his orders. "Mac, find a bird," she repeated several times, hoping he would remember his lessons. "Good boy. Move out! Find a bird!" She let go and gestured him ahead. The dog leaped away, head down and docked tail wagging.

He found some interesting scent, paused, and fell into the classic point position. Elsie hurried up to him, patted him without saying a word, and went to her knee beside him to see what had his attention. All she could spot was an orange salamander wriggling its way along the forest floor. Mac whined and nudged her hand. She raised a warning finger and refused to give him a treat. "Find a bird," she ordered again, rising and sending him off.

This went on for nearly an hour. Mac found more deer droppings, a pile of fox scat, several frogs, and an empty eggshell. Elsie responded, "Leave it!" to each of them. She snapped the leash back on him and they started back toward the hay meadow. They picked up the mowed lane again and followed it where it led alongside another of the ubiquitous stone walls, under the shade of old oaks and sugar maples. The day grew warmer. Elsie was thinking about returning to the car when Mac came to a sudden stop and pointed. Taking every precaution to make no noise, she poked at the tufts of grass with her walking stick. The dog quivered.

"Whoa," she ordered under her breath and poked some more.

Mac couldn't stand it anymore. He sprang ahead into the young grass at the foot of the wall, pulling the leash out of her hand. A small brown bird erupted from her nest. She started to flutter as if her wing were broken, but when Mac got too close, she lifted in flight and headed into the wood. Mac, too inexperienced to know better, took off after her, leash flapping behind him.

Elsie yelled to him, but he was too excited to heed her. He didn't even respond to the dog whistle she'd been using to call him. Off he went, deeper into the wood, with Elsie losing ground at every step.

Angry now, she stopped and caught her breath. He was supposed to return to her. They'd been practicing it; she thought he understood. Oh, well, in the excitement of the chase anything could happen, especially with a young dog. She called aloud, and off in the distance, she heard him bark. "Mac, come!" she shouted, making her voice as stern as she could.

Whether it was his training or his fear at being out in the open alone that brought him back Elsie never knew, but after far too long a time, he showed up and sat at her feet. She had to pat and praise him for returning, especially if she wanted him to associate returns with good things, but it was obvious he needed a lot more practice in the woods.

Elsie decided they'd had enough for one day and turned back to where she thought the lane was. Somehow, however, they'd gotten turned around, and they walked a much longer way out of the wood than they had into it. When the land fell away to the west she realized she was going in the wrong direction. She turned around to retrace her steps. But the paths didn't seem to go where she remembered, and she found herself following a faint track northward. It wound around some glacial erratics and dipped into a slight depression before becoming clearer and bending to the east, where she wanted to go. She decided to stay on it for a while.

Before long she came upon signs that someone maintained the track now and then: a downed tree had been cleared to the side, and low branches trimmed. It must be a snowmobile track, she thought, and then she remembered the landowner mentioning such a track that crossed the road a bit farther on from where she had parked. She stepped out with more confidence.

Mac tugged on the leash, and she let him move ahead of her. The ground grew a little damp, and he was happy looking for frogs. They rounded a curve and came to a group of erratics, left by the last glacier. Six or seven large rocks clumped together on a bit of high ground, with trees growing among them and an alder bog on the far side. Elsie decided she needed a rest, so she called Mac to her side and found a comfortable place to sit.

She had water and an apple in her fanny pack. She gnawed on the apple, tossing the core away when she was done. Mac watched her eat but didn't quite beg. She gave him a drink and a doggie cookie. The rocks looked familiar somehow, but she couldn't think why. She shrugged. New England was thick with miscellaneous boulders dropped by glaciers. The thought amused her—glacier droppings, deer droppings. Sue would appreciate the humor.

It was getting later than she had planned. She got to her feet and moved on. The track did end at the road, perhaps three quarters of a mile farther on. It was marked with one of those little snowmobile club signs to help riders find it. She turned right onto the road and found her car after only five minutes' walk. Mac made no objections to jumping into the truck; he flopped down with his head on his paws. Elsie wished she could let someone else do the driving as she headed for home.

Chapter Eleven

Brush & Bevel was empty of customers, which was fortunate for them. Whenever she felt unsettled, Ginny rearranged things. At home, she rearranged furniture. At work, she rearranged paintings. At the moment every picture in the gallery was propped up against a wall or a divider, awaiting her decision on where to put it. She stood in front of the window, looking toward the back of the shop to imagine how it would look if she grouped all the artists in alphabetical order.

That was silly, she told herself. That would put the Anton Siberutes next to the Froma Salopeks, and the two clashed in color, style, and subject. They would look awful next to each other. It would also put Bourne's wild animal portraits and Berger's landscapes together, which wouldn't look quite so bad, but it would still form an unhappy pairing. All right, forget the alphabet. Stupid idea, anyway.

Ginny was tempted to pull all the Bergers together and feature them in the center section, where they would catch the eye as customers walked in. She decided against it, since she would need to do that later, once she had a definitive identification of the nude as a lost Berger painting.

Jerry Berger. Part of her itched to put it on display right now. Another part, the savvy businesswoman part, urged her to wait until she had all the cards in her hand—provenance, price, permission to make prints—before she hung it publicly. A tiny but loud part of her wanted to tear it from the stretchers and burn it. Damn, she could use a drink!

No, not at work.

The framing workload was light, so she'd given both her employees the day off. She didn't work alone often, and she missed her staff. She knew Elsie had plans to take her husband's dog out for training in the woods and who knew where Sue might be. Maybe out on her bike or tramping around down by the river. At any rate, Ginny was alone for the day. It looked to be a quiet one, too, with no customers coming in. She began shuffling prints around to see where they would show to best effect.

Just when she couldn't stand being alone any more, Mark Horner from the Chowdah Bowl stuck his head in the door. "Hey, I'm going fishing! Want to come?"

The absurdity of the proposal was just what she needed. "With you? On a boat? Not in this lifetime!"

He was always inviting her out on his beloved fishing boat, and she was forever refusing him. She had no desire to go out to sea with him or anyone else, or to catch big fish, which inevitably entailed nasty things like cleaning them. Besides, she was sure she'd get seasick.

He caught something in her tone and walked the rest of his body into the room. "Are you okay? You look upset."

She brushed her hair out of her eyes and found a smile for him. "Look at this mess. Of course I'm upset!"

He looked around. "You're right. It's a mess. But

you do this at least three times a month. Why does today have you so upset?"

She opened her mouth to explain, but nothing came out. After all this time, did she really intend to confess her long-ago affair to a fishmonger? No, that was unfair; Mark was a good person and much more than a seller of fish. Under the cover of his mocking laugh, he was always available when she needed help. She knew she could count on him in disagreements with the landlord, and she was glad the Chowdah Bowl lay between her shop and Jemmie's. Too bad about Mark's two ex-wives.

"Are you worried about Jemmie? He's been much quieter since DiAndreo talked to him."

"Not really. He's more silly than scary. He gives me the creeps. No, it's something else, Mark. I can't talk about it yet."

"Good gossip?" His eyes lit up with delight. "About somebody I know?"

She laughed. "No, not at all. Don't worry, you'll know as soon as I can tell you. Thanks for stopping in. I guess I was just feeling lonely."

He gave her a concerned look, and then made the best offer he could. "I'll send over some chowdah. You haven't eaten lunch, have you?" He spun on his heel and strode out.

No, she hadn't eaten, but that was the least of it. Mark was kind, in his own rough way, and she was grateful to him. But she still had this mess to clean up, and she still had to deal with the nude and her complicated feelings about it. She went back to work, stopping only when a bewildered teen dropped off a bowl of clam chowder complete with oyster crackers.

No doubt about it, she felt better after eating.

So she felt fortified when the phone rang. Without any premonition, she lifted the receiver and answered in the normal way. "Hello, Brush and Bevel."

"Is this Ginny Brent?" asked a rough-voiced man with a strong accent.

"Yes."

"I got a note heah to call you about my bah," he went on, dropping his r's in the classic New England style. "I'm outta business now, but what can I do f'ya?"

Ginny sat down hard on a chair. "You got my name from North Shore Sales?"

"Yuh. Mitch says ya wanted a name of some painteh fellah?''

"Yes. Yes, thank you for calling. What did you say your name was?"

"I didn't, but it's Jack Morgan. I used ta own Cap'n Billy's down on the Cape. All the drunks useta call me Cap'n, but I never went ta sea. I figger, I don't need ta be a sailor ta serve booze."

Ginny laughed in spite of herself. "No, Jack, you don't. About this painting—"

"See, that's the trouble. I only bought Billy's about three yeahs back, lock, stock, and barrel, as they say. Even came with a cah, would ya believe. It didn't run fer shit, but it was a cah. Anyway, if theah was a painting, it was theah when I bought the place. I nevah put anything like that up."

Ginny deflated. "Oh. Well, then, I'm afraid—"

"Mitch says you're looking fer a gift fer your husband, that right?"

"Yes."

"And ya sent him a little tip fer his help?"

"Yes," she agreed with a sinking heart. How much was this going to cost her? "I could do the same for you."

"'Cept I don't know about any ahtist. Tell ya who might, though."

"Really?"

"No shit. The guy I bought the bah from, he knew all that type up in Provincetown."

"What's his name? I'll give him a call."

"He might not remember, now."

"Doesn't matter, Jack. I'll just try anyway."

"Matt Baldwin. I dunno if this number's still good, it's kinda old." Jack recited it for her and grunted when she read it back to him. "That's it. I oughta warn ya, he's a crazy old coot. Sold the bah 'cause he got religion. Least that's what he said. I think he sold it 'cause he couldn't make a livin' at it. I sure as hell couldn't. Damn drunks."

Well, Ginny thought, it was less than she wanted but more than she hoped for. She tucked the scribbled number into her briefcase and went back to work, very much heartened.

Chapter Twelve

Although Sue Bradley would have enjoyed riding her bike or tramping around down by the river, which she was wont to do whenever her day off coincided with good weather, she indulged in neither passion. Despite the sunny, mild weather and the temptation of a spring hike, she made other plans. Yaneque's visit and the mysterious oil painting had piqued her interest, so she called an acquaintance she had at the weekly paper that served the Temple Mountain area and made an appointment to use its archives.

The *Town Crier* was just moving into the computer age, so most of the archives were still on microfiche. Some of the very oldest issues, old enough to qualify as genuine antiques, were still on actual newsprint, carefully preserved in special clear envelopes. Sue didn't need to go back that far, however. She was interested in two stories that went back ten years.

Her contact was Jim Cooper, a hyperactive reporter who attended most of the board meetings in the neighboring towns. He signed her in and led her down the stairs to a basement room that should have been damp but wasn't, though it smelled of old dust and disuse.

"You're lucky I'm here today," he said. "Just had to come in to meet with the editor. We're planning a big story on the new conservation land, and we needed to touch base and look at some maps together. Anyway, here you are. You know how to work these machines? Put the fiche in the holder here, and slide this handle back and forth, up and down, till you find what you need."

"How do I pick out a particular story?"

"You know the date?"

"Not precisely. It was winter, ten years ago."

"Good enough," Jim said. He ran his finger down a line of cabinet drawers and opened one, riffling through the cards inside until he found the appropriate envelope. "Here you go. November, December, January. If that's not the right one, just look in here for the next one, or the one before, whatever you need. Don't put anything away, though. We have an intern who does that, and he goes crazy when he finds things out of place. Can't blame him, I suppose. Anything else? Oh, the water cooler's upstairs, sorry about that. So's the ladies' room. All set?"

"I got it, Jim. Thanks a lot. See you around sometime, right?"

He bustled away, and Sue sat down with a sigh. Such a lovely day outside, and here in this basement, she couldn't even look out a window, since there were none. She set her notebook and pen to one side and tested the motion of the handle. It was so easy to work that she had to remember to slow her movements in order to keep the type on the screen readable.

It didn't take her long to figure out the system. The microfiche was set up almost like a book; each page of the newspaper was displayed in its entirety, though only a part of it showed on the screen at any one time. Moving the handle up and down let her read from top to bottom of the page. If she moved the handle to the right, she could move to page two, page three, and so on to the end of the issue, and then on to the next week. A leftward move took her back to the previous page or issue. It was like a time machine, she thought, spinning through the month in a single motion. The whimsy delighted her.

It was tempting to read through the pages one by one; old stories that tickled her memory jumped out at her and begged for her attention. The fire at the Churchville general store; kids rescued after they tried to cross the river on thin ice; the perpetual debate over the placement of new roads. Preparations for the big Thanksgiving parade that traditionally got rained out brought a sad smile to her face. Only two years ago, the long-time organizer had died, and no one stepped up to take her place. The parade faded into the past. Maybe someone would start it up again this year.

Enough of that. Sue took a firm grip on the handle and edged forward a couple of weeks, searching for stories about a big snowstorm. She knew it had happened before Christmas, because Yaneque had mentioned she'd been released from the hospital in time to put up her tree. An accident with a logging truck and a delivery van on top of the pass would surely have rated some kind of story. Maybe not page one, but something.

Ah, there it was. The accident didn't rate page one, but the snowstorm did. A large picture of an impressive snowplow hurling a wave of snow took up the top third of the page in the December 8 edition of the *Crier*.

Second Storm in Two Weeks Dumps Eight Inches
Temple Pass Closed

The second significant storm of the season dropped up to eight inches of snow on parts of the Monadnock region Tuesday. State and local crews worked all day and into the night to clear roads already lined with high banks of cleared snow from previous storms. Most schools and many businesses closed early or did not open at all.

The storm followed close on the heels of an earlier storm that produced ten inches at the weather station atop Pack Monadnock. Police reported numerous minor accidents in all the towns, with one major accident that left a driver hospitalized and closed the highway over Temple Mountain. (Story, page 3.)

Sue scrolled on and found the story on page three. There was no picture of the accident, but Yaneque's business photo was featured.

Local Businesswoman Seriously Injured

Yaneque Duprey, owner of RunAround, a courier service, suffered serious injuries when she lost control of her vehicle at the pass on Temple Mountain during the snowstorm Monday. Police report a logging truck jackknifed on the eastern slope of the pass, just below the old ski resort. Duprey was not able to stop in time to avoid hitting logs that had spilled off the truck. She was taken by ambulance to a hospital in Nashua, where she is recovering from head injuries. The driver of the logging truck was not injured.

State police report Duprey was the last car permitted over the pass before they closed the road. "All the rain was turning to sleet and snow," said Trooper Dan Thompson. "The road iced up real quick, and the snow was falling on top of it. It was getting pretty hard to see, too, so we made the decision to close."

Duprey's vehicle overturned and was completely destroyed.

The Temple Mountain Pass is often closed in bad weather. Because of its altitude and its location across a long ridge, precipitation there changes to ice or snow before it does in lower areas, leading to the decision several years ago to maintain plowing and sanding units on both approaches to the pass. The eastern unit was able to reach the site of the accident first and provided sanding for the Douglass ambulance.

"Well, that was not very informative." It didn't add much to what she already knew. But then, she hadn't expected much information. What interested her most happened after Christmas. She scrolled on, past the holiday ads, stories about charitable funds, and the usual New Year's Resolutions editorials. Nothing much changed from year to year, it seemed.

Until she reached the January 12 edition of the *Crier.* It was a shock to come across Jerry Berger's photo, the same as on the website, plastered on the front page. This time the headline screamed at her in large print.

Local Artist, Model, Found Dead by Hunters

Two hunters came upon a grisly scene in Harpersville last weekend when they were out tracking a wounded deer. Fresh snow partly covered the remains of a man and woman.

One of the hunters, Alan Jones, remained at the scene while the other, Charles Currier, hiked back to their car and called for help. Currier then guided the police to the scene.

"They'd been there a few days," Jones said. "Long

enough for coyotes to get at them."

There was no identification with the bodies, but they have since been identified through dental records as that of Jerry Berger, a well-known local artist, and Abby Bingham of Mill Falls, who sometimes posed for him.

They had been reported missing last month after the December 6 snowstorm. Foul play was suspected when Bingham's car was discovered in Keene. Berger's car has not been found.

Abby Bingham was the wife of Michael Bingham, an alderman in Mill Falls. He was arrested last month on charges of threatening an employee at Brush & Bevel, an art gallery in Westford.

The bodies were discovered behind a stone wall in the trees uphill from Justa Road. It is a popular hunting area, but is not visible from the road.

Because of the deep snow, police had to use snowmobiles to reach the site and to remove the bodies. They worked at the scene most of Saturday and part of Sunday to recover body parts.

"I have seen a lot of bodies coyotes have chewed on," said Currier. "But it's different when it's people. It was awful."

Cause of death has not been determined. "They were out there at least three weeks," said medical examiner Cheryl Stetson. "Wild animals had pulled body parts a distance away. It will be some time before we can say what killed them."

"The state police major crimes unit was called to the scene and transported the bodies to Concord," Stetson said. The state attorney general's office was also consulted.

It is not known why Berger and Bingham were in Harpersville, or how they arrived in the woods where they were found. Only indoor clothing was found in the vicinity.

Mrs. Bingham was well known in Mill Falls for her community activities, including her support for better schools and her charitable organizing. Berger had gained regional and some national attention for his artwork, particularly the series of paintings called "One Year."

Funeral arrangements will be announced.

"Well, that was pretty gruesome," Sue told herself. Even sanitized for the weekly paper, there was no avoiding the image of dismembered, half-eaten bodies in the snow. There was even the discreet hint of illicit goings-on between the two victims, and the righteous anger of the wronged husband. Or was she reading too much into it?

Sue got to her feet and went upstairs for a drink of water. Jim was nowhere to be seen, but she didn't expect to find him. She wondered if any of the current reporters had been with the paper ten years ago, and if they would talk to her about the story. Caution overtook her; if she asked about Berger, they would want to know why, and she certainly couldn't tell them about the painting. Not yet. Besides, Ginny would want to control the announcement of a rediscovered painting by Jerry Berger.

On she scrolled, making weeks pass in seconds. If only she could do that when she was sick or the weather was bad! She found the obituaries and the funeral announcements, and the brief related story about Mike Bingham stepping down from his position as alderman while he served his probation. Well into the next fiche, buried on page nine of a mid-April issue, she came across the story that reported the police determination.

Deaths Were Murder/Suicide

State police have completed their investigation into the deaths of Abby Bingham and Jerry Berger, whose bodies were discovered in January in the snow in Harpersville. Both were shot in an apparent murder/suicide. "The condition of the bodies made it difficult to determine the circumstances of the deaths," reported Anna Fitzgerald, of the NH State Police. "However, we believe Mrs. Bingham was killed by Mr. Berger, who then killed himself."

Asked if a suicide note had been found, Fitzgerald said only that the investigation was continuing. She had no explanation for why the bodies were discovered in indoor clothing during the winter.

Berger's brother Howard said he did not believe his brother committed suicide. "Jerry was a happy guy. His career as an artist was blossoming, and no one who knew him saw any hints of unhappiness. As for his killing Abby (Bingham), that's completely ridiculous. He wouldn't harm a fly."

Mike Bingham, husband of Abby Bingham, did not respond to requests for an interview. A spokesman for his office read a statement, "Mr. Bingham still mourns the loss of his wife. He is satisfied with the result of the police investigation and wishes to commend them for their hard work. Nonetheless, the fact remains his wife is dead. She is and will be greatly missed."

A retrospective of Berger's work is planned for next month at Brush & Bevel in Westford.

And that seemed to be the end of it. Sue put the

fiches into their envelopes and started to put them back in the drawer before she remembered Jim's warning about the intern. She set them on the table, and then peeked into the drawer again, wondering if the next fiche would have any more information. She'd already spent most of the morning here, and her stomach reminded her it was time to eat lunch. She should go home and enjoy the rest of the spring day.

But her finger was still in the drawer where the fiche belonged. She glanced at the next envelope. It was clearly out of order, almost a year later. Curious, she put it into the viewer and scrolled through, keeping a casual eye open for any of the names in the stories she'd been reading.

All she found, however, was an ongoing investigation into certain tax irregularities in Mill Falls, which, according to what she read, were threatening to cause problems for the town of Douglass. She didn't bother to read the whole story—it was long in the past and it didn't concern her hometown—but it had something to do with auto registrations assigned to the wrong town.

She replaced the fiche in its envelope, closed down the reader, and went upstairs.

Jim had already gone out to interview people on the street for their views on the proposed land conservation project, so Sue left a note of thanks for him. She included a wry mention that she supported the project, but her vote didn't count since she lived two towns over.

It was still early enough, she thought, to get a bike ride in during the afternoon. She could always do the laundry another time. As she headed home, she realized she would pass the place where Yaneque had run into the logging truck. On a whim she decided to stop and poke around.

The old ski resort had been deserted for a number of years, and new growth blurred the once-smooth slopes. The T-bars and the chairlifts had long since been sold or vandalized. Rugosa roses and blackberry brambles covered the old parking areas.

Sue parked off the edge of the road, near the trailhead that led north and south along the ridge. She liked that trail, but had never completed its twenty-seven-mile length at one go. She had enjoyed several short hikes along the trail, often marked with weird cairns and opening onto magnificent views of Mount Monadnock. Someday she would manage the whole trip.

Though she poked up and down the roadside for quite a distance, she never found any signs of that long-ago accident. She wondered if Yaneque had ever done the same thing.

What would it be like to lose a part of your life like that? To have a hole in your memory? There were plenty of things Sue couldn't recall at will, but that was simple forgetting. To know you left home one morning and woke up in the hospital two days later, with absolutely no memory of the time in between—very unsettling.

There was a lot of litter on the side of the road, most of it food wrappers and drink bottles. People were slobs. What would it cost them to take their trash home and dispose of it as they should?

Sue bent to examine a chunk of rusted metal that caught her eye. It looked like a brake caliper. She fantasized that it had something to do with RunAround. Not likely, of course; the Rotary Club cleaned up the road along here twice a year. After ten years, would even a caliper endure? She dropped it back to the ground, brushed off her hands, and went home.

Chapter Thirteen

The next Tuesday was the one day every week when Ginny and her two employees were all at work. The rest of the time they split up the schedule, with some combination of two of them taking care of business most days. They looked forward to being together each week. It was a chance to consult with each other on difficult framing projects, plans for promotions and advertising, and other bits of information to keep Brush & Bevel up-to-date and moving forward. Often enough they indulged in personal chat, too, keeping each other posted on what was happening in their lives.

"How did Mac do yesterday?" Ginny asked Elsie.

"Oh, he wasn't bad. We flushed a grouse, and then he got all excited and ran after it. We got a little lost, but we found our way back to the car all right. He just needs more work."

"Did he find a lot of frogs?"

Elsie laughed. "Yeah, he's a real frog dog. There was a big puddle with a bunch of frog eggs in it, and he went splashing through there like a herd of buffalo. Those egg masses are so sticky! He was filthy when we got home. It took me an hour to clean him up."

The other two women sympathized. They both had grown sons, and remembered all too well the messes that adolescent boys of any species could get into. For a while their talk drifted to the vagaries of the young, then they returned to business.

They reviewed several work orders that had minor variations from the norm—a V-groove here, a double opening there, the need to deckle the edge of a watercolor—as well as some tricky mounting for a silk scarf. Ginny preferred to mount textiles as close to square as possible, while Sue argued for the natural flow and drape of silk. As usual, they ended up with a compromise. Sue would mount the scarf square at the top but allow it to hang a bit loose along the edges and bottom, tacked down just enough to keep it from blousing out and touching the glass.

Elsie and Ginny discussed the difficulties of mounting a thick section of newspaper in such a way that sometime in the future it could be taken from the frame to read the inside pages. Elsie suggested she could build up a "nest" around the section before putting the mat over the front page. Ginny thought it was a good solution, and they agreed to cut a sample mat before ordering the frame.

"This needlepoint," Sue began, holding up what was supposed to become a pillow top.

"Ugh, that's so skewed!" Elsie shook her head. "It'll take forever to block."

"That's Trina Murphy's, and she wants it by next week," Ginny added.

Sue groaned. "No way. She should know by now that it takes time to get her things straightened out. Two weeks minimum, plus another week if she decides to frame it instead."

Ginny frowned but accepted the inevitable before going on to the next problem. "Do you think you can work on the Berger piece today?" she asked Sue.

"It's on my list. Did you find out any more about where it came from?"

With a rueful shake of her head, Ginny expressed her regret. "Only a little. Jenna Rudolph gave me the number of the auction house, and through them I got in touch with the man who sold the bar where it used to hang. But when he bought the bar it was already hanging there, and he had no idea where it came from."

"Dead end?" Sue winced at the inadvertent pun.

Ginny didn't seem to notice. "He gave me the name of the owner before him, but the phone number he gave me seems to be out of date. I'll try again. I have some contacts on the Cape; maybe somebody knows where he is."

"You could try the booze distributors, too. They might remember."

Ginny made a face. "My cover story would be a little thin with them. I've been saying I want to find the artist to get a present for my husband. I think it would be stretching it to keep looking beyond the bar owners."

"Have you googled the ex-owner?"

Her eyebrows rose. "Now why didn't I think of that?"

"State liquor commission? Local police?"

"You're stretching again."

"Not if you tell the truth," Sue insisted. "That it involves a famous artist and a lost painting."

"Hmm. The trouble is, I don't want to get rumors started about this thing. At least not until we know for sure it is his work. So get it cleaned, would you?"

Sue gave her a mock salute. "Aye, sir. But if we get a signature out of it, would you need to have provenance?"

"It wouldn't be as critical. But you know me. I like to have all my ducks in a row. Besides, I'm curious. Aren't you?"

Sue grinned. "I'm so curious that I went out to Douglass and spent all morning yesterday looking at microfiches in their archives. Not a fun way to spend a beautiful spring morning."

"Did you learn anything?"

"Only that Jerry and Abby were wearing indoor clothes when they were found. And they never found Jerry's car. And one other thing, though I don't think it's related: do you know why Mike Bingham left New Hampshire?"

That required some thinking. "Let me see. He served his probation—"

"And he resigned as alderman after his arrest for scaring Elsie."

"That's right. I think his insurance business went downhill after that. I mean, would you buy insurance from somebody who waves a gun around at a harmless woman? Anyway, I remember that he told everyone he didn't want to live around here anymore because it reminded him too much of Abby."

"He had an insurance agency?"

"Or he worked for one."

"What was he like?" Sue wondered, delighted at getting so many answers.

"Mike? He was good-looking, I guess. Loud. Insurance salesman type, you know what I mean? Flashy dresser, always had a big diamond ring on his pinky. In fact, I think that's how Abby got acquainted with us. Mike used to buy her jewelry at Jemmie's, and then she started coming over herself to pick things out or get them repaired. Then one day she looked in our window and liked the Edward Gordon prints, and from there—" she shrugged to indicate Sue knew the rest of the story. She made a shooing motion. "I've got to get some work done. Go find me a Jerry Berger signature underneath all that smoke and grease."

****

Sue clattered down the stairs with Elsie, but something in Ginny's words awoke some very strange thoughts in her fertile imagination. Could there possibly be a connection between insurance fraud and improperly assigned vehicle registrations? She'd have to think about that.

Elsie started on the newspaper framing while Sue got the painting out of storage and made preparations for cleaning it. She liked this part of her job, as long as she could have fresh air while she did it. The cleaning solution had a pungent odor. She took the painting, the solution, and a supply of soft clean cloths and cotton swabs into the common area of the basement where she set them on a small table next to the garage door, which she opened wide to let the stink disperse. She made sure the screen was in place to keep the bugs—and frogs—outside. Selecting a cloth, she moistened it with cleaner and began the slow, circular motion that would remove accumulated soil, dust, and grease.

The process was always the same, but the results were unpredictable. Sometimes what seemed to be a soiled painting turned out to be just a dark one, and no amount of cleaning could brighten it. Other times, cleaning offered surprises: the staff still marveled at the three ships revealed in the background of a seaside painting, and the cheerful yellows that had been dull gold flowers in a floral. Sue half-expected something to show up in this painting, given what little they knew of its history. Imagine, an original Jerry Berger hanging in a bar.

The lower left corner produced nothing more than a general lightening, so Sue folded the cloth to a clean spot and worked toward the top in an inch-wide strip. When she reached the top, she moved the cloth over an inch and worked down, always rubbing lightly in small circles. Once she had cleaned the entire surface vertically, she would repeat the process on the horizontal, paying special attention to the nooks and crannies of the paint itself. The repetitious movement gave the task a peaceful, trance-like feeling. Sometimes she got so engrossed in this work that she let the rest of the world drift out of her awareness.

The first vertical pass revealed nothing except that what appeared to be mud at the base of the rocks was, in fact, mud. Sue took extra time to clean it away, using cotton swabs with the same gentle, circular motion.

"How long has that door been open?" screamed a voice in her ear, rising to near-panic pitch.

Sue started and jostled the bottle of cleaner. She grabbed it before it could fall over and spill its odorous contents on the table and floor. "Dammit, Jemmie! There's a screen and I've been here the whole time. Trust me, no frickin' frogs got in." *Where the heck did he come from?*

"*I* snuck up on you," he roared. Then, with a visible effort, he made a placatory motion. "Sorry. I'm sorry. I keep telling myself that frogs have no teeth." He showed his own teeth in a nervous grin—a man facing up to his fears. "I still have to check. What are you working on?" His voice trembled with forced politeness.

Sue tried to shield the painting from view, but Jemmie stepped close and reached for it. She moved one of the cloths to cover the nude woman and slid the painting away from his reach. "It's a customer's piece," she began, but then she saw Jemmie's face. He turned a ghastly shade of paste, and then flushed so dark she feared he might burst a blood vessel.

"She's dead!" He pointed a shaky finger at the model. "He killed her! Oh, God, she's dead!"

Sue leaped to her feet and yelled for Elsie. "Yes, of course, Jemmie." She grasped his arm and spoke soothingly. "It was a long time ago. It's okay, Jemmie, relax."

"He killed her! Out in the snow!"

Sue frowned. Why was this death so vivid to him? "Who killed her? Do you know?"

Elsie skidded into view, the phone in one hand and a box cutter in the other. Sue gave her a small signal with her hand, trying to let her know she shouldn't interfere. Jemmie, lost in the past, didn't seem to hear her question, but he was calming down, taking a visible hold on himself.

He forced an apology out between clenched teeth. Shudders still passed through him. "Sorry. It was that artist, wasn't it? That's what the papers said. The artist killed her."

"Did you know her?" Sue kept her voice soft to calm him.

Jemmie drew a deep breath, as if he was waking from a nightmare. "I knew her. She was a customer. So pretty. I designed a few pieces for her. Wonderful lady. Great taste. Such a shock. Such a shame."

"It was," Sue agreed, though she hadn't known either of the victims. Elsie gestured with the phone as if to call for help, but Sue gave a shake of her head. "Are you okay now, Jemmie?"

He shuddered, but his voice was stronger. "I'm fine, fine. I'm—I'm sorry I scared you, Sue. Um—just close the door?"

She patted his arm. "I'll be working out here for a while yet, and then I'll let the fumes air out, but I promise I'll close the door, Jemmie."

He straightened his broad shoulders, gave her a nod, and stumbled away. He couldn't resist a backward glance.

"Whew!" Elsie whistled. "That was too close! Are you okay?"

Sue nodded, thinking hard as she watched his retreating back. "I'm okay, Elsie. I'm glad you were here. He certainly reacted strangely to this painting."

"We should tell Ginny about it."

"You better believe it."

"She's with a customer right now. I heard the doorbell just before Jemmie came over."

Sue sighed. "I'd better get back to this before he freaks out again. Let me know when Ginny's free."

Elsie returned to the newspaper piece, and Sue picked up her cleaning cloth. Her hand was shaking. She put the cloth down again and took some deep breaths while she thought. Why should Jemmie get so hyper about a painting of a long-dead customer? Why should he insist, "He killed her"? He was a bundle of surprises, no doubt about that. She considered his frog obsession, and the way he yelled at his staff. For a moment there, Sue had felt really threatened. If Elsie hadn't been present... She shrugged. Jemmie yelled a lot, but he hadn't ever hurt anyone. So why did she keep thinking about all those sharp things? Maybe she'd better talk to Ginny about that, too.

She sighed again and returned to her work. She began the horizontal cleaning now, working methodically from left to right. The foreground was thick with paint, and she used a lot more cotton swabs to be sure she removed all the grime stuck in the brushstrokes. They came away gray or brown with grease and smoke, and the painting began to brighten up. There were more colors among the leaves and underbrush, and even the rocks began to glow. And sure enough, Jerry's signature, as clear as could be, showed up in the lower right.

"Elsie! I found the signature!" Her coworker dashed up, with more confidence this time, and examined the cleaned patch.

"Well, I'm not the expert, but that sure looks like his signature. I'm getting Ginny, whether she's with a customer or not."

In short order, Ginny clattered down the stairs behind Elsie, breathless in her excitement. Sue rotated the painting to reveal the signature. Ginny leaned over it and studied it for a long moment. Her finger reached out and traced the air above the letters.

"Ginny?" Elsie murmured. "What do you think?"

She raised her head and tore her eyes from the painting. "I think," she said in a strained voice. She cleared her throat and began again. "I think we have it. I'm sure now. Jerry Berger painted this picture." She straightened and seemed for a moment to look inward, and then she shook herself. "That's great. I was pretty sure before, but this clinches it. Wow! This is wonderful. Good work, Sue. It looks so much better. Is there much more to do?"

"I just want to finish the horizontal pass. There was a lot of muck here in the bottom, so I need to make sure I got it all out. And…" she hesitated.

"Yes?" Ginny prompted.

Sue told her about Jemmie and his reaction. Elsie commented that he'd seemed very subdued when he left. Ginny shook her head.

"Well, there's nothing we can do about him. Finish up, Sue, and let me know when you're done. I'll want to call Jenna in then."

As Ginny headed upstairs and Elsie went back to her project, Sue bent to the job again. As she moved higher on the image, she uncovered a series of reddish dots and strokes, incongruous against the grayish granite rocks. There was even a puddle of red underneath an alder bush emerging from the murk on the right side of the painting. Could Jerry have meant to add in some additional color in those places? How odd that he hadn't finished them. Or maybe, she considered, he'd been about to change something, but she couldn't imagine what it could be.

At last she reached the top of the painting and sat back to look at it from a distance. No hidden squirrels popped out from the trees, nor any herons stalking fish in the distant pond. Only that line of red. It led from Abby's outstretched right hand, down the rocks, across the ground, and under the alders. Sue's scalp prickled. What could it mean? She lowered her head until her nose almost touched the paint. She peered at the drops below the hand and caught her breath.

"Elsie? Would you bring the magnifying glass out here, please?"

"What is it?" Her colleague peered over her shoulder. "Did you find something else?"

Sue pointed to the red dots and strokes in the middle of the picture. "Yeah, but it's weird. I want to look at these red bits." She chose a spot and put the glass above it, straining her eyes to see better. She muttered something under her breath, poked with a tentative swab, then looked under the bushes. She handed the glass to Elsie. "What do you see?"

Elsie wiped the glass with a finger and looked. She moved it away and looked at the unmagnified bit, wiped the glass more thoroughly with a corner of cloth, and looked again. "I think the red stuff was added later," she said in a low voice. "What do you think?"

"I think you're right. It looks like it might be watercolor paste." The face she lifted to Elsie was pale. "I think Jerry was trying to tell the world something. I think it's supposed to be blood."

"Should we take it off?"

Sue chewed her lip. Her impulse was to forge ahead and clean off the red substance, but she thought better of it. "I want a witness to this. Let's leave it on for now, and get Ginny down here. And maybe Tom DiAndreo."

"You think it means something?"

"At the very least I want him to witness the condition of the painting before we go any further. And we should get some photos, too."

Chapter Fourteen

Less than an hour later, Ginny looked at the cleaned painting again and agreed the red stuff had been added after the picture was completed. She didn't think much of it, however, and it was only after thinking about Jemmie's reaction that she consented to call in Tom DiAndreo. She didn't believe it was urgent, though, so when Tom suggested an appointment a week later she didn't argue. She agreed to take some photos before, during, and after cleaning off the red stuff. Sue already had done photos before and during the cleaning, as a matter of course. It was often stunning to see the differences between a soiled piece of art and the cleaned one. Customers liked to keep a copy of the "before" picture for themselves.

After admiring the cleaning job Sue had done, Elsie kept thinking she had seen the painting before. That was impossible, of course. Ginny's research proved it had hung in a bar on Cape Cod for years. Elsie seldom went to the Cape and wouldn't have gone to a bar if she did. And even if she'd gone to a bar, she wouldn't have paid much attention to a nude since she didn't care for them.

The rest of the day was taken up with the normal tasks of the business. Elsie worked on the newspaper framing and got caught up in the old headlines. Her own memories of the Nixon's resignation in 1974 were rather vague. She'd been busy raising a family back then and didn't have much interest in politics. Even now her natural reserve meant she seldom expressed her opinions about what was going on in the world, although she knew she held very different views from Sue's. One of the underpinnings of their relationship was not needing to discuss their differences in the political arena.

She and Sue speculated a little bit about the Berger as they worked. They had no more doubts as to its authorship, so they ruminated on its value. They wondered how much the Rudolphs had paid for it at auction, and if they would permit prints to be made of it. Sue claimed she wanted a print to commemorate their part in its recovery.

"I wonder if it has a name?" Elsie mused.

They toyed with that idea for a while, proposing titles from the somber to the silly. Woodsy Woman? Abby's Ass? Dame au Naturel? Frog Pond? Pink Lady on the Rocks? Cap'n Billy's Broad? In the end, they accepted that the heirs, Jerry's brother and sister, would claim naming rights, although they might take suggestions from Jenna and Bob Rudolph. Still, it was fun to think about.

****

"I wonder why Jemmie had such a reaction to the painting," Sue said later, as she was pinning a piece of counted cross stitch.

"Didn't he say she was a customer of his?"

"Yeah, and Ginny said Mike was, too. He started buying Abby's jewelry from Jemmie, and then she came over here, and came into Brush & Bevel. That's how she met Jerry. Did you know him, Elsie?"

Elsie stored the newspaper project in the bin where they kept matted items until their frames come in. She wrote the frame moulding number and the dimensions on the order form for the proper vendor while she thought about Sue's question. "Not very well. I only started working here, oh, about a year before he died. He was nice enough. Ginny liked him a lot. He was kind of a flirt."

"Really? Did he flirt with you?"

"Oh, a little. Not really a flirt, just a guy who liked to talk. Once you got him started on his work, you couldn't shut him up. He'd go on all day about it. One time he and Bert Boucher were here at the same time, and you should have heard them! Bert's an artist, too, you know, and they just went on and on about different kinds of paint, and they argued about giclées. They were just coming out back then, and the ink wasn't very stable, but the colors were so good a lot of artists put up with it for the sake of the color."

"Funny how things work. Now they're telling us giclées are good for at least two hundred years. And they sure do look good."

Elsie agreed. "Now if they can just figure out how to make digital photos with a stable finish, that would be great."

"There was a guy in yesterday who said he knows of a giclée printer that can print up to two feet by three feet. I almost asked him about the finish, but he's a new customer and I didn't want to overwhelm him. If he ever brings a piece in—" Sue broke off, looking at her co-worker, who had started to frown and tap her finger against her lip. She did that sometimes when she was dredging up a memory. "What is it, Elsie?"

"I'm not sure; I'm trying to remember something. I think…can we get the Berger painting out again?"

"Sure." Sue went over to the locked cabinet where they kept very valuable pieces and keyed in the locking code while Elsie cleared a space on the work table. Lifting the painting out with her usual care, she set it down like a holy relic. "It sure cleaned up pretty," Sue said.

Elsie made a noncommittal sound. Sue noticed she was very careful not to look at Abby's body. Sue didn't mind tasteful nudes like this one. Abby had struck a graceful pose, leaning on one of the gray rocks, with her back to the viewer. The woman had a rather large bottom, but it was nicely shaped, firm and smooth. Her arm, as she pointed down and to the right, concealed all but a hint of the swell of her breasts. Sue could wish for such a nice shape for herself. She admired the curve of Abby's back, the rich black waves of her hair, and the lovely oval of her face. The expression on the face was rather troubled. While Sue was cleaning the piece, she had focused on the actual paint to make sure she removed all the dirt and grease. Now that she could step back a bit, she saw things she hadn't seen before. Abby's dark eyebrows drew together over her nose, and the corners of her mouth were turned down just the slightest bit. The effect was one of worry or anxiety, very much at odds with the beautiful setting. Sue supposed the patrons of Cap'n Billy's didn't bother much with the setting or the model's emotions, however well they were depicted. No doubt they fixated on—

"That's it!" Elsie cried, pointing. "I know where that rock is!"

She indicated the boulder that hid Abby's feet. It was a typical, gray granite boulder, with flecks of sparkly mica and a vein of white quartz. The vein split the rock in a way that was vaguely reminiscent of buttocks, Sue thought with a private grin. "You know where it is?"

"I think so," Elsie replied, not quite so sure of herself. "I think it looks an awful lot like the rocks where I was hunting with Mac yesterday. I can't be positive, of course, and there are rocks all over New Hampshire, but when I was there yesterday I remember thinking it looked familiar."

"Hmm. Could you find it again?"

Elsie dithered. "I think so. It shouldn't be too hard. We could take one of the photos of the painting to be sure."

"Was there a lake or a pond in the background? Was the ground boggy?"

"It was boggy. I don't know if there was a pond, I wasn't looking. When could we go?"

That was a problem, because Sue and Elsie seldom had a day off together. They were still mulling it over when Ginny came downstairs with some new framing orders. She noticed the Berger painting on the table and the serious looks on their faces.

"What's wrong?" she asked in alarm.

"Nothing, nothing," they hastened to assure her. "It's fine."

She fanned herself with her hand. "Because if this got messed up…"

"We haven't touched it, honest. Don't worry."

"All right then. So why do you have it out?"

Elsie hesitated, then began, "Well, yesterday I was

out in the woods training Maculato, and when he flushed a grouse, he took off instead of waiting for me. We got a little lost, but then we came upon what looked like an old town road the snowmobilers use. So we went along that for a while. It led us to a pile of rocks that looks an awful lot like this." She gestured at the painting. "Except nobody was there, of course."

Ginny chewed her lip. "And, of course, you two want to check it out, right?"

Elsie made a tentative suggestion. "Field trip?" In the past, field trips had been scheduled several times a year and always involved some sort of connection with art. Lately, however, the gallery had been too busy to be able to close for an entire day.

"We haven't done a field trip in a long time, have we? I don't want to close…could you and Sue do this by yourselves?"

Sue spoke up. "Frankly, Ginny, I'm scared of this one. I mean, you know I hike by myself all the time, but this is spooky. Going to the site of a murdered artist's last work—well, it makes me nervous."

"And you'd feel better with *me* along?" Ginny's laugh held a nervous note. "I don't want to go tramping through damp woods, with bugs and brambles and all that. I'd probably catch poison ivy or fall into a cellar hole or something. Or the bears would eat me!"

Elsie didn't catch the humor in Ginny's voice and responded only to her fear. "Oh, we wouldn't have to go the way Mac and I did. We could find the other end of the snowmobile trail and walk in from the road. It's not very far going that way. We could take along one of the photos to compare it."

"Well, that would be very interesting, but what's

the point?" Ginny asked. "If we knew the site of the work it would add to the promotion, but it's really not necessary."

"It's not just that." Sue spread the words out as if she were afraid to say them. "It's the red stuff on top of the paint. I think Jerry was trying to tell us something, something very awful. I don't think we should go alone."

Ginny raised her head. "What are you saying, Sue?" Elsie just stared.

"I think we should take the police."

"The police! Whatever for? If you think it's that dangerous, why go at all?"

Sue chewed her lip. "Well, aren't you curious? It's such a neat puzzle. Besides, I'm always up for a walk in the woods. I just think it's a little spooky that Elsie found this location. And I have this feeling there's something else going on, too. I don't know what, but maybe we'd find the answers in the woods. It shouldn't be all that dangerous."

"We could take Mac," Elsie suggested. "He's such a goofball, though, he'd probably slobber all over any bad guys."

The laughter that comment inspired eased some of the tension. Ginny looked at Sue. "What could Jerry possibly have been trying to tell us?"

"If it was murder, did he know who might have wanted to kill him? And why? If it was murder/suicide, what was his motive? Was he having an affair with Abby and she was going to break it off? Was Mike a jealous husband? And why, why, why did Jerry paint that line of red?"

"Those are good questions for the police to ask,"

Elsie said.

They looked at the painting again. Ginny drew her finger down the red marks, as if she could read them like Braille. "I think we'd better clean this off."

"Not now," Sue insisted. "I want Tom DiAndreo here."

Ginny looked at her steadily. "All right. I'll call him. Right now?"

"No time like the present," said Sue, but her voice shook.

Chapter Fifteen

Tom DiAndreo was relieved to be called to Brush & Bevel again. He sat slouched behind his desk at the Westford police station, deep in a drawn-out discussion with his future in-laws about some small detail of the wedding that didn't make much sense to him. How could they expect to get a wedding photo framed before the wedding? And why did they seem to think he had such a photo? So he was quite happy to get off the phone with them and attend to police business when the switchboard buzzed him.

"I've got to go," he told Donna's mother politely but with just enough urgency to convey the idea he was very busy. "I'll call you when I get off duty."

He switched to the interoffice phone. "DiAndreo." He listened for a moment. "In plain clothes? For a painting? What the hell do they think is going on?"

What the desk told him then made him jump to his feet. "The Berger case? You tell them I'll be there in, oh, less than five minutes. No, wait, if they want plain clothes they don't want a siren going. Tell them ten, then. Right."

Standing behind the closed door of his miniscule office, he shucked his uniform and changed into the still-damp clothes he'd worn to work this morning. They exuded an unpleasant aroma, since he'd worn them for his workout earlier, but they'd have to do. He resisted the urge to slap the emergency beacon on the roof of his battered car as he drove out of the historic town center and down the busy highway that sliced Westford in two. It wouldn't do to announce his arrival if there was a situation going on.

Despite his sense of urgency, he forced himself to keep to a sedate pace as he parked around the corner from Brush & Bevel and strolled to their door, the gun under his arm a reassuring weight. The request for plain clothes roused his sense of danger and self-preservation. He cast a wary glance into the gallery before he pulled open the door. Ginny was seated before her computer, seeming quite unconcerned. He relaxed a fraction and went in, still on the alert. His eyes flicked from her face to the space behind the wing chairs, to the restroom door that stood ajar as usual, to the displays of frame samples.

"That was quick," Ginny said by way of greeting. "I didn't expect you here so soon."

"Are you okay?" he asked, concern making his voice rough.

"What? Oh, yes, we're fine," Ginny said without any stress that he could detect. "Didn't they tell you that? I'm sorry if we alarmed you..."

Tom let out a breath and rotated his shoulders to relax them. "The desk said you wanted me in plain clothes. I was worried about Jemmie Demarais."

Ginny tsked. "I told them plain clothes would be okay." She stressed the last word. "I meant there was no call for alarms and sirens and stuff. I guess I wasn't clear enough. I'm sorry."

He took another deep breath and gave himself a mental shake. "Everything is really all right?"

Ginny assured him again there was no cause for alarm. "We've discovered an unknown painting by Jerry Berger," she went on to explain.

His interest spiked at the name. "Berger? Isn't he the guy involved in that murder/suicide years ago? And the model's husband came here looking for him?"

"Yes, that's right." Ginny sounded surprised.

"I looked it up in the files after that meeting we had here. For some reason, I wondered if there was a connection with Jemmie's Gems."

"Well, the model used to shop at Jemmie's, that's all I know. Anyway, we cleaned it, and there is something rather odd about it. We wanted to have an impartial witness here when we take off the last bit of— well, it's not really dirt, is it?"

"I think you'd better let me see it."

She led the way downstairs to the workshop, explaining as she went. "A customer brought this piece in a few days ago. It's a nude, only the second one Jerry ever completed as far as I know. The model is Abby Bingham. We think we know where it was painted."

"So?" DiAndreo didn't have much interest in art, even if it was a nude done by a man thought to have killed the model and then himself. Why would Brush & Bevel call him about where it was made?

Ginny turned to face him when they reached the bottom of the stairs and spoke in a low voice, as if she didn't want to be overheard. "So, we think it was painted just before they died, and my employees think it might hold some clues to their deaths. We thought you might be interested."

"You thought right," he agreed with a sheepish grin. The adrenaline rush faded, leaving a sour taste in his mouth, but he was glad now that he had come.

She ushered him into the main workspace, where Sue and Elsie had cleared the table. He immediately focused on the rather small painting they were bending over. "What's the red stuff?"

"We think it's a thin wash of watercolor paste," Elsie replied. "At least, it responds to water."

"What's underneath it?"

"That's what we want to find out." Sue's voice was firm but he detected a trace of anxiety underneath the firmness. "Would you close the door, please?"

Ginny objected. "You usually want it open, Sue. What's up?"

Sue shrugged. "Just a bit nervous, I guess."

Tom obliged her, then returned to the table. "Explain as you go along," he requested.

Elsie began the explanation. "We've already cleaned the painting with a standard cleaning and conditioning fluid. Sue usually does that, because the smell really bothers me. It was filthy. See?" She displayed the cloths Sue had used, which were indeed grimy. "It was hanging in a bar for years and had gotten covered with grease and smoke."

He grunted. "Did you find anything else on it?"

"Mud." Sue shrugged. "There was mud all over the bottom part of the picture." She swept her hand across the area where the mud had been. "I had to clean it out with cotton swabs."

"Did you save them?"

"I did." She indicated a pile of swabs, all filthy gray. He picked one up by its middle and peered at its ends.

"Looks like fine sand, ordinary mud. The lab might

be able to get something out of this."

"After ten years?" Ginny was incredulous.

"You'd be surprised," was all he said. "So you cleaned it. You didn't happen to take a picture of it before you cleaned it, did you?"

Elsie nodded. "We always do. It's fun to see how different it looks before and after."

"Nothing else showed up?"

"Just the red stuff. Oh, and Jerry's signature."

He whistled in appreciation before he bent over the painting, mumbling thanks for the magnifier Ginny stuck in his hand. "The red stuff sure looks like an addition, right down to the fine brush marks in it. But then, an artist would have fine brushes, wouldn't he?"

"Could it be anything else?"

The women looked at each other. "Gesso," Ginny ventured. "It could be colored gesso."

"Would an artist have it on hand?"

"Most artists do. It's used as a primer for canvas, among other things. We keep it on hand to repair damage to carved frames, rather like plaster of Paris."

While she was speaking, Elsie fetched the jar of gesso from the other room. She spread a dollop of it on a scrap piece of mat board. She showed Tom how, with a palette knife, she could create a three-dimensional effect, and then she smeared the gesso into a thin layer to let it dry.

DiAndreo dabbed a clean wet swab onto the gesso and watched for an effect. The gesso thinned out, but left a gritty residue. "We'll try it again once it dries. In the meantime, let's see what we get when we take a little of the red off the painting."

With another clean swab, Sue wiped a tiny drop of

water onto the paint in an unobtrusive spot. If this process seemed likely to damage Jerry's work, at least the effect would be minimal. After a pause to allow the water to soak in, she picked up a fresh swab and gently wiped away the red drop. It thinned out, leaving a pale wash of white behind. Sue repeated the process with another pair of swabs, and the paint underneath was revealed. It was a dark brownish red that blended into the stems of the underbrush.

Ginny let out the breath she had been holding and checked the picture with the magnifying glass. "There seems to be no damage, no softening or discoloration of the paint," she murmured. Sue and Elsie sighed with relief.

"I think we can go ahead," Ginny said, "but be careful. Take as much time as you need. I don't care if it takes the rest of the week, I don't want this work damaged."

Tom made a gesture of caution. "Hold on a moment. I think you should hold off on cleaning any more. If this does have any bearing on the Berger/Bingham case, we don't want to jeopardize it by removing evidence."

Ginny flushed. "This painting is far too valuable to be stuck in a police evidence room. It just won't do."

He raised his hand to calm her. "I'm not saying that. Just don't go any further with it until I get back to you, all right?"

The three women looked at each other. "Well, I guess it goes back into the safe." Elsie sounded a bit relieved.

"One more thing. You say you know where this is?" Tom indicated the pile of rocks in the picture.

"I'm pretty sure of it," Elsie replied. "I was out training my dog yesterday, and we ended up someplace that looks a lot like this. This stone is rather distinctive." She blushed as she pointed to the one that reminded Sue of buttocks.

Tom considered it and then grinned. "Cops get paid to be nosy. Could you take me there?"

"We were going to ask you to go along," Sue said in relief. "We thought it would be a good idea to have an impartial observer with us."

"You weren't going to go alone?" His eyes were wide in alarm.

They exchanged guilty glances.

"I see. You were, weren't you?" He shook his head and thought about it. "Well, I really can't stop you. I'd just feel better if I went along, too. Besides, I don't have anything going on tomorrow, and this would be a good excuse to avoid any more phone calls from my future mother-in-law."

Sue looked eager. "Can we go tomorrow? It's my day off, but Elsie is supposed to work."

They turned to Ginny. "I can't do it tomorrow. I have two appointments with customers. But you don't really need me, do you? Why don't you go, both of you? Go with Tom. I'll be fine here by myself."

There was a little more discussion, but in the end they agreed to meet at Elsie's house in the morning. She could even take Mac along for more training.

"Keep that picture safe," Tom said in parting. "And don't toss the rags or the swabs. I'll get an evidence kit from my car and take them back to the office with me. I don't think it would be a good idea to discuss this adventure with anyone else. Agreed?"

Ginny offered him a cup of coffee, to which he agreed after a quick consultation with his conscience, and they returned upstairs. While she prepared it, he wandered around the gallery looking at the framed art. He leafed through the brochure of Berger's works, stopping to admire *A Walk in the Rain* and several other prints. He wondered if there would be room in his new condo for one or two of them, and if he could afford them.

Ginny handed him a mug. "What can I sell you?" she asked with good humor.

He smiled and took a sip. "What would something like that one downstairs go for?" To his surprise she took him seriously.

"That's a good question. A new painting by an artist of his stature—he's not right on the top rung, you know, but he's very well respected and his prints still sell well. A couple of his pieces are in significant museums, and I think his reputation will only grow with this piece. The new owners paid a pittance for it, the lucky ducks. Somebody didn't know what they were selling."

"So how do you put a price on it? I assume they'll at least want to insure it, if not sell it?"

She sat down and began to explain it to him. "The biggest obstacle is determining for sure it is one of Jerry's. The signature, the fact Abby never modeled for anyone else, and my own assessment settle that question. I'll probably ask Pam and Howard, his sister and brother, to check in their archives to see if they can find any studies or photos that show the work in progress, just to be sure."

"There's an archive?"

Ginny smiled. "Sort of. The original paintings, at least the ones Pam and Howard control, are in Howard's house in New York. Pam lives in Jerry's old place out in Douglass, and whatever was in the studio is packed up in boxes in her upstairs. It's quite safe there; we spent a lot of time sorting and packing things properly. The room is part of the house, so it's climate-controlled. I haven't been there in a couple of years. All the paintings have been scanned and stored electronically so it's easy to print what we want to." She hesitated. "Do you know about fine art prints? Limited editions and so on?"

"Ginny, I don't know a watercolor from an oil."

"Okay." She settled deeper in her chair. "You have the original painting, right? In Jerry's case, they're now selling for tens of thousands of dollars."

"That much?" Tom was surprised.

"The original of *Birch Meadow* recently sold for thirty-two thousand, and it's not one of his best. So the answer to your first question, how much would the nude sell for, is probably between twenty-five and forty thousand. You can't tell until it actually goes on the market."

He whistled. "Well, I guess I won't be buying it! Go ahead and tell me about prints. Like posters?"

"We've only done *One Year* as a poster, because it's so popular. The limited edition, signed and numbered prints of that one are going for about twenty-five hundred. A limited edition," she went on before he could ask, "is just what it sounds like. A limited number of very high-quality prints, usually between two hundred and a thousand, are made on high-grade paper. They're usually a different size than the original, and they are signed and numbered by the artist. They're fairly high priced and can become quite valuable. Sometimes, especially now that the process is more stable, an edition of canvas prints is made, too. Smaller number of prints, higher price. In either case, no more prints of that size are ever going to be made. They break the mold, so to speak. Okay so far?"

Tom nodded, and Ginny continued. "The artist can, if he chooses, use the same image for other purposes. For instance, one artist we sell had a fairly large edition of fine art prints of one of her pieces, and then she also licensed a part of the image for note cards, calendars, mugs, and so on."

"I see. All kinds of ways to make money from art."

Ginny laughed. "It only works for a very few. Some of the best ones only do very high-end prints and make a very good living. Others do better with the licensed products and make a pretty good living. Most artists starve."

"And people like you make a living off the artists. Oh, don't get upset," he forestalled her. "I can see where artists need you to sell their stuff. Marketing is a job all in itself, from what I hear, and not everyone is good at it."

"I'd much rather see a good painter have the time to work with their art, rather than at selling."

They sipped at their coffee for a few minutes in silence. Then he asked, "Is it important to have a chain of custody in art? In my field, we have to prove a certain item we hand in to court is the same one we picked up at the crime scene. We call that a chain of custody, and it's crucial sometimes."

Ginny smiled. "We call it provenance. Knowing

where something came from. Yes, it can be important. Sometimes the stories that go along with the art are just as important as the art itself. Like the Hope Diamond, for instance, with all the so-called curses on it."

"Or the Curse of the Pharaoh?"

"Yes, like that." Ginny laughed. "In this case, we know so far that it was hanging in a bar, and we know how it got to the current owners. We just don't know how it got from Jerry to the bar. Now that we have the signature it's not critical, but it sure would be nice to know."

DiAndreo was beginning to think he really should get back to his office when a sudden racket arose two doors down at Jemmie's Gems. Ginny rolled her eyes. "He's at it again. Damn, and he's been so good ever since you talked to him."

He listened to the crescendo of shouting. Jemmie's voice rose higher in pitch and volume, and enough words could be distinguished Tom felt the need to shut him up. He feigned nonchalance. "I think I'll take a stroll down there. Thanks for the coffee."

Chapter Sixteen

Elsie had coffee ready when Sue and Tom DiAndreo arrived at her house the next morning, dressed for hiking on a damp spring day. They tossed waterproof boots into Elsie's truck in anticipation of mud puddles and stuffed rain gear into their backpacks. At least, they agreed, rain would keep the omnipresent bugs down.

Maculato was beside himself with excitement at meeting all the new people and could hardly settle down long enough for Elsie to put a leash on him. His whole body wiggled as he greeted Tom and licked his hand. Then he danced over to Sue.

"He's gotten so big since the last time I saw him, Elsie. Look, I don't even have to bend down to pet him. Will he get much bigger?" Mac recognized her friendly voice and pressed his head against her hip. Sue smiled at him and patted him between the ears.

"I hope not. He's almost too tall for his breed. We're hoping to put him to stud in a couple of years. Come on, Mac, up you go." Elsie all but shoved him into his crate.

Tom was to follow in his personal car. "I don't have any jurisdiction in Douglass, so I talked to the chief over there. He said to call him if we discover anything, but he's pretty sure the case is cold. My chief thinks I'm just stirring up old gossip, but he's willing to stretch a point and let me go with you on the strength of the painting. Especially since I'm off duty. Just so we're clear—if anything turns up, I take over until the Douglass police arrive, okay?"

The two women agreed, grateful for his company. They felt safer with him on this expedition. Elsie gave him detailed directions in case they got separated. She and Sue climbed into the truck and headed out. It was a straight run west for about twenty miles on the main highway, over Temple Mountain, then north into and beyond Douglass on a back road. The trip would take about forty-five minutes.

They were carrying several photos of the Berger painting in various stages of cleaning. As they drove, they studied them and speculated on what, if anything, they might find.

"Bags of gold and jewels," Elsie suggested dreamily.

"Or some pictures of them being naughty," said Sue, bringing them down to earth.

"Romantic letters."

"Blackmail."

"A lock of hair from each of them."

"A dead baby."

"Sue!" Elsie protested in a shocked voice. "Anyway, Abby couldn't have kids, remember?"

"Oh, yeah, that's right. Well, we won't know until we get there. If there even is anything to find. It might've been just some allegorical allusion. And anyway, it's been ten years. There might be nothing left. I wonder what Tom thinks about it."

****

Tom DiAndreo, meanwhile, was trying to decide

the very same thing. He'd always been intrigued by puzzles—one reason he decided to go into law enforcement was the chance to solve crimes and mysteries—but he didn't expect much from this outing. If there were anything to find, it would probably be some tawdry lovers' memento. Didn't artists always have affairs with their models? He had very little experience with artists, but he shared the common misconception they were all flighty, morally questionable, and a bit mad. Take that Van Gogh guy, who cut off his own ear. What normal person would do something like that?

He yawned and stretched his long legs as much as he could while he drove. After talking to Ginny yesterday, he'd gone back to the files at the cop shop and had stayed far too late studying them. During his workout this morning, he thought so hard about what he'd found, he did too many reps on the leg lift and his muscles were aching.

The rain started to fall as they approached the Temple Mountain pass. Tom switched on his headlights and wipers and grumbled to himself. He was having second thoughts about tramping through the wet woods on a wild goose chase just to verify that a certain painting was painted in a certain place. As interesting as that might be to art lovers and historians, it was no part of a policeman's business. So why was he going along?

He sighed. In part because he was nosy, but also because he wanted to have an investigation going when he switched over to the state police after the wedding. Although he would have to pay his dues for a couple of years in the form of highway patrol work, he planned to take every opportunity he found to become a detective.

In the meantime, he intended to nose around and perhaps push the Major Crimes Unit into reopening this case.

He looked forward to the change from small-town crime and small-town politics. As a detective in the state police, he would have access to far more interesting cases and far more comprehensive facilities. He would be less limited by jurisdictional disputes— though such disputes were endless and universal. In a case like this one, for instance, he would be able use his state badge to talk to officials in Douglass, where the suicide used to live, as well as to their counterparts in Harpersville, where the bodies were discovered, and in Mill Falls, where the murder victim had lived with her husband.

Then he considered Ginny's conviction that Berger was not a suicide, but a murder victim. Ginny Brent seemed to be a good judge of character, even though he suspected she had something of a drinking problem. He'd seen enough closet drinkers to recognize that slight skewing of the way she looked at the world. Or maybe that was just because she worked in the art field. Perhaps anyone who dealt with the depiction of reality, instead of reality itself, was just a little bit screwy. Still, Ginny seemed positive Berger wouldn't have killed himself. So did Elsie. Both of them had known the artist, so Tom was willing to grant them some sort of insight into Berger's character. Sue agreed with them, but she hadn't known Berger and based her belief on an analysis of his paintings, which seemed pretty thin to Tom.

Near the top of the pass, Tom swerved to avoid hitting the parked car of one of the volunteers cleaning up the litter. Miserable bastards, he thought with sympathy. Horrible day for a job like that. But he was grateful to them for the work they did each spring and fall. Without them, the roadsides of New Hampshire would be far messier.

Ahead of him, Elsie's jeep signaled as she slowed to make the right turn. They descended into heavier rain and wisps of fog. Another car, one of those ubiquitous small sport wagons, turned behind him and then pulled up into one of the driveways. Elsie slowed as she followed the twisting road, and Tom could see her pointing out landmarks to Sue as she drove. She waved out her window as they passed a barway into an open field and continued up the road a bit more to another break in the stone wall. Here a snowmobile sign marked a trail crossing, and Elsie parked just beyond it.

Tom pulled up behind her and trudged around to his trunk for his rain gear. "Think it'll get any worse?" he asked as he pulled on his boots.

Sue stuck her head into a poncho and then, to his surprise, pulled an umbrella out of her backpack. She noticed his reaction and shrugged. "I know, it looks silly to walk through the woods with an umbrella, but it works. At least, on a clear trail it does. I wouldn't use it to bushwhack or on a steep trail where I'd need both hands to climb. Up Mt. Monadnock, for instance, or on some of the trails in the White Mountains. Snowmobile trails are usually wide and pretty well cleared, though, so this should be okay. Elsie says it'll only take about twenty minutes to walk in to the rocks." She grinned at him with a twinkle in her eye. "I've got a thermos of hot tea for when we come back. Maybe I should have brought something to spice it up!"

Elsie had donned her own rain gear and was getting the dog out of the crate. He strained to be free of the lead and put his head down to sniff. "Mac, heel," Elsie ordered. He whined but obeyed, sitting down at her feet. They all pressed against the truck as a vehicle sped past, sending a spray of water against them.

Sue laughed. "Well, we might as well start out wet."

Tom frowned. Was that the same sport wagon that had followed him onto this road and pulled into the driveway? He hadn't paid much attention to it at the time, and it was gone too quickly for him to note the plate. Probably nothing to worry about. He didn't mention it to the ladies.

Elsie led the way across the road and onto the trail. The dog nosed around at the end of the leash, excited by all the woodsy smells. He scared up a few frogs who weren't much bothered by the rain, but that was all. Even the chipmunks and the squirrels were snug in their dens in the stone walls.

The rain grew heavier as they slogged on. The trail became muddy in some places, and once or twice they detoured around deep churned-up areas where the snowmobiles had disturbed the forest duff. Sue complained about the destruction they created.

Several times Tom, bringing up the rear, stopped and looked behind him. He couldn't see very far through the young leaves. It was raining hard enough now to cover the sounds of their footsteps. The dog didn't seem to be aware of anyone except the three of them. Tom took some comfort in that. Then again, he reminded himself, Mac was a bird dog who was doing his duty in earnest. When they reached a meadow Elsie released him from the lead with a wide, sweeping gesture. "Mac, find a bird. Find a bird," she said, and the dog took off.

Waiting for Mac and skirting mud puddles took up a bit more time than planned. It was just over half an hour before they reached the pile of boulders Elsie remembered. The rain had slowed again, but the fog was thicker, lending a kind of otherworldliness to the scene. They could barely make out the pond in the distance. "I wonder if that's the heron rookery I've heard about," Sue murmured. "I'll have to check it out sometime."

They circled the rocks several times before they were sure that this was indeed the site of the Berger painting. The artist had changed the perspective and altered the appearance of several of the stones, notably the one with the strip of quartz in it. The real-world stone was much smaller and the resemblance to buttocks was far less pronounced. Sue made a disappointed sound, but she didn't say anything.

Elsie pulled a photo out of a pocket. The three of them consulted under Sue's umbrella.

Tom looked from the rocks to the photo and back. "I think you're right. I think this is where the painting was done, or at least this was the setting. I can't imagine making someone pose nude in here. She would've been eaten up by mosquitoes and black flies in no time. This is a regular bug factory with all the water all around."

Elsie made a wry face. "Mac likes it. He's supposed to be a bird dog, but he'd much rather chase frogs." She called but the dog was out of sight. She shrugged. "He'll come back soon. At least he's learned that much."

Sue held up the photo at arm's length, trying to gauge where Abby had stood. She handed Elsie a camera. "I'll have to climb up there. Tell me when I'm in the right place."

Elsie took the umbrella and set it aside, then watched as Sue clambered around the rocks. "A little more to the right," she called, when her co-worker had reached the top. "That's it!"

Sue leaned against a boulder and struck a pose. "The rain gear makes the picture, doesn't it? Can't you just see someone wanting to pose nude here? What a lark!" She studied her surroundings and extended a hand. "Is this the way she's pointing?"

Elsie and Tom studied the picture. "I think so," Tom said. "Just past that rock under your hand. That's it. Like she's pointing into the bushes there. Wait, I'll get a picture." The camera flashed.

Sue bent down to look at the ground. "Where does the line of red go? Tell me when I'm close."

"Warm," Elsie cried, as in the old children's game. "Warm, no, cold…okay, warmer. You're getting close. It disappears for a bit, then it comes out near that bush."

"Okay." Sue scrambled between two stones and half-slid down to the base of the pile. "I can see the way water would flow through here, so I guess that's how blood would go, too. Right under that alder bush." The others joined her as she poked among the red-brown stems of the alder.

Tom scuffed at the mud with a boot. "I wonder if they buried something here. After ten years, it's hard to tell."

Sue said, "I'm thinking about those stories in the

newspaper, the ones I looked up. What if Jerry and Abby came back here? After the painting was done, I mean?" Tom looked dubious and she hurried to go on. "Or maybe it was just Jerry that came back. What if he found out something he wasn't supposed to know and wanted to hide the evidence?"

"Like what?"

"I don't know. Something about Mike, maybe?"

Elsie stared at her. "And then he put that red stuff on the painting as a clue? Does that make sense?" She examined two of the photos side by side and then moved deeper into the thicket. She poked with her foot, moving mud aside. A few minutes later she gave a cry and held up a small stone between her fingers. It bore traces of red paint.

Sue hurried to her side. "Are there more?" She dug around with a foot. Tom broke off a branch and began probing the soil. He hit several stones and roots, and produced more red-painted stones. He sought out a flattish rock and started to dig seriously, moving the mud aside.

"The ground is awfully soft here," he muttered. "Wait, ladies. Stand back and let me dig." Before long he had a wet hole about two feet deep. His rock scraped against something metallic. "Ah," he sighed and set aside the rock in favor of scooping with his hands. With a long sucking sound, an old cash box appeared. "Somebody get a picture of this. Get several. I'm going to open it. Let me have the umbrella."

The box yielded to his efforts and revealed a package wrapped in some kind of oilcloth and sealed in a plastic bag. Tom opened the bag and folded back the cloth to reveal a stack of papers. "They look like receipts or something," he said.

"I'll take that," came a loud but shaky voice.

Jemmie Demarais stood behind them. The gun in his hand didn't shake, and it was pointed straight at them.

Chapter Seventeen

Back at Brush & Bevel, Ginny congratulated herself. She had used the quiet day engendered by the rain to catch up on some paperwork, and then without much hope she tried to find a current phone number for Matt Baldwin, the previous owner of Cap'n Billy's. Without knowing his address, Directory Assistance couldn't assist her, and she didn't think she'd get anywhere if she called the liquor distributors or the local licensing boards. Then she recalled Sue's suggestion about using the Internet. *Well, why not;* she typed the outdated number into the virtual Yellow Pages.

Bingo. The old number yielded Baldwin's address and armed with that she tried Directory Assistance again. She bypassed the automated response and spoke to a live operator, who read out the new phone number as if he'd waited all day to do just that. Ginny dialed it, her heart beating hard in her chest.

Six rings, seven, eight. She resigned herself to talking to an answering machine and was already rehearsing her spiel when a smoke-roughened voice croaked, "Hello?"

"Am I speaking to Matt Baldwin?" she asked as politely as she could.

"What's it to ya?" It came out as a cough.

Ginny decided on a direct approach. "My name is

Ginny Brent. I own an art gallery in New Hampshire. I'm looking for information concerning a painting that used to hang in Cap'n Billy's. There may be a reward involved."

She could almost feel the man's attention snap to her. "Yeah, this is Baldwin. What painting?"

"Do you remember the one of a woman among some rocks?"

His answering cackle grated in her ear. "Ah, yeah, the big ass. What about it?"

The need for careful handling was obvious. "That painting was done by a well known artist, Mr. Baldwin. I think I could guarantee you a reward if you can help us find out how it got to that bar." *The "us" was a nice touch.* Well, it wasn't a complete lie; she was sure the Rudolphs would be interested, as would Jerry's sister and brother.

"Humph. I dunno, it was a long time ago."

"Well, I know you sold the bar about three years ago. Are you enjoying your retirement?"

He grumbled deep in his throat. "Hell, no. Time I paid off all the creditors, there warn't two coins to rub together. I been scrapin' by on odd jobs and cussedness ever since." He coughed again, a nasty rasping sound. "I might be able to help ya out fer a thousand bucks."

Ginny laughed. "He's not that famous a painter. Two hundred."

"Five."

"Two fifty. I don't absolutely have to have this information, you see. I can do just fine without it. It would be icing on the cake."

"Three hundred, and I'll remember all about it."

"Fine," Ginny agreed, though she would have gone

to five hundred. "Tell me what you know."

"Money first."

Ginny sighed. "Tell you what. You call Mitch at North Shore Auctions, and then you call Jack Morgan, who bought the bar, and you ask them if they got their money. Then you call me back and we'll do business." She gave him all the phone numbers and made him repeat them. "The sooner the better," she suggested.

"You bet your ass," he snarled, then hung up.

Not the most pleasant character to deal with. He knew something about the provenance of the painting, that much was clear. Ginny just hoped it was worth the money she would have to pay him. There was nothing she could do about it until he called back, so she returned to her paperwork.

Unfortunately, she couldn't get her mind to focus on it. She closed her eyes and thought about the painting again. With her characteristic honesty, she realized she just didn't want to accept the idea of Jerry being with Abby. The stab of pain caught her by surprise. In ten years, why hadn't she gotten over him?

To her relief, Baldwin returned her call in less than an hour. The scratchy voice bruised her eardrum. "Seems like you're legit. Send me the money and I'll send back the dirt."

She laughed at him. "Yeah, right. Tell me what you know now. I'll send half right away and the rest if it checks out."

"Shit, woman, you don't want much."

"As I said, I don't really need—"

"All right, all right. This guy walks in about six, seven years ago—make it eight, it was the summer we had a hurricane hit here—he walks in with this thing under his arm. 'My wife won't let me keep it,' he says. He says, 'Put it over the bar and I'll come visit my lady friend every night.' So I put it up there. Filled a hole, see? And that's all I know."

"The man's name? And where did he get it?"

"Aah…Chris, that's all I know, I swear. He said he found it on the side of the road. I ask you, what a bunch of bull. He swore blue it was the truth, but I never believed him."

"This Chris—was he local? Did he live on the Cape?

"Nah, he was summer people. Lived up in N'Hampsha someplace. And don't ask me where, I swear I dunno. No, wait, there's somethin' else. He was in the Rotary, y'know? He used to talk about joining up here when he retired."

"What happened to him?"

She could almost see Baldwin shrug. "How should I know? He didn't show up the last summer I had Billy's, so I didn't feel bad about selling his bare-assed lady. This is really a famous artist?"

"I'll invite you to the unveiling, Matt."

"Fuck you, lady. I ain't got no car. Just send me my money." The phone slammed down in her ear, and Ginny chuckled. *He is just like my father, no class whatsoever.*

Still, she owed him something. She was a little further on. A Rotarian named Chris, from New Hampshire, who summered on the Cape. There shouldn't be more than, oh say, fifty men who met that description. Matt would get his first payment of hundred and fifty, but probably no more.

Chapter Eighteen

Tom DiAndreo thought fast. He judged the distance between him and Jemmie, factored in the complication that he was squatting in slippery mud, and plotted the positions of the two women with him. All three of them were in Jemmie's line of fire. Tom had learned from bitter experience not to discount a desperate man's aim.

There was no doubt Jemmie was desperate, despite his quavering voice. He had a haunted look about him. His eyes darted from side to side, though he never moved his head. *How did he manage to sneak up on us? He must be more experienced in the woods than he looks*. Adrenaline stabbed at Tom; if Jemmie had experience in the woods and a gun to add to his habitual barely-controlled anxiety, he was even more dangerous than Tom had ever imagined.

"Hey, Jemmie," he said, keeping his voice even and calm. "Let's take this real easy, okay? I'm going to put this stuff back in the box. Then I'm going to stand up. Is that okay with you?"

"Keep your hands up—I want to see your hands all the time. Got that, cop?" Jemmie tried to sound tough, but his shaky voice spoiled the effect.

Tom moved with great care, inch by inch. He bent his head to the stack of papers and folded the oil cloth over them. While his head was down and his face was hidden from Jemmie, he whispered to the women, "Don't do anything. Don't look at him. Watch me. When I stand up, I want you to run. Elsie, behind the rocks. Sue, into the trees. Don't look back. Keep moving. Got it?" He lifted his eyes without moving his head and glanced into their white, frightened faces. "Whatever you do, don't come back without help." He finished wrapping the papers and tucked them into the box. "I don't understand what the problem is, Jemmie. These just look like old receipts. What's the big deal?"

"They're mine, that's the big deal. They're mine. They belong to me and I want them back. I gotta get them back!" The jeweler's voice rose into the upper registers. His breath rasped in his throat. "Hurry up. It's fuckin' cold out here."

"The ladies are going to stand up, Jemmie." Tom used his voice to soothe the man. "It's cold and wet here, and I don't want them to fall. Is that okay with you? If they stand up?"

Jemmie waved the gun. "I-I'm sorry you're here," he stammered. He almost seemed to mean it. "Go ahead and stand up. But don't move, see. I swear I'll shoot."

Tom gestured with his hand. Sue and Elsie unbent slowly from their crouch. They kept their hands at their sides and their eyes on Tom as they took a step or two backward.

"Don't move, I said!" Jemmie screamed. "Don't move anywhere!"

"It's okay, Jemmie," Tom soothed him. "You should see the mud here, they had to get some footing. Is it okay if I stand up now?"

"Give me the box." Jemmie held out his hand. Again he made the gesture with the gun.

Maybe he isn't so experienced with firearms. Tom put his hands on his knees and began to straighten his back. Still bent over, he reached for the box, glancing over his shoulder to judge his aim at Jemmie. Then he stood to his full height.

Several things happened very fast. Sue and Elsie darted in opposite directions, their sudden movement a surprise even to Tom. Jemmie waved the gun from side to side without firing. Maculato, a white and brown blur, leaped from behind the rocks and propelled himself straight at Jemmie. A stern female voice yelled, "Leave it!" The dog rose up on his hind legs and deposited something in Jemmie's outstretched hand before bounding away.

Jemmie screamed. The gun went off. Tom heaved the box in Jemmie's direction and launched a tackle at him. Sue, yelling like a banshee, swung her hiking stick as if it were a baseball bat.

Had Jemmie still been standing, the stick would have hit him square on the temple. It might have knocked him out if it had connected. Instead it whistled through the air and just missed Tom's head, still tucked low for the tackle. At the end of his leap, Tom fell on Jemmie, who scrabbled on the ground squealing as if he feared for his life. Sue wound up her arm for another blow; Elsie caught up the gun in one hand and attempted to latch onto her dog's collar with the other.

"Get it off!" Jemmie pleaded, twisting under the weight of Tom's body. "Get it off!" He screamed again, in complete panic. The dog thought this was a marvelous game and bounced around the struggling men, barking for all he was worth. Jemmie covered his face with his hands and convulsed on the ground. *"Get it off me*!"

Tom twirled him onto his belly and pressed a knee into his neck. Sue plopped herself on his thrashing legs, while Elsie managed to capture Maculato and drag him away. Incredibly, she still had the gun in her hand. Even more incredibly, she seemed to know what to do with it. She held it pointed down and away from her body.

Tom wrenched Jemmie's right arm behind his back, then his left. He shifted his weight so that his knee pressed into Jemmie's spine. "Something to tie him, quick," he panted.

Elsie slipped her fingers into Mac's collar and handed over his leash. Tom looped the braided leather around Jemmie's unresisting wrists. "Please get it off," the jeweler moaned, shuddering. He made no move to try to escape either Tom or Sue.

Keeping his knee in position, Tom nodded to Sue to rise. She eased herself to her feet and then, to Tom's surprise, removed her belt and fastened it around Jemmie's ankles. He nodded his approval, slid off the subdued man, and rolled him to his side.

A frog hopped out from under him. Mac barked at it.

Jemmie cringed. "Get it away from me! Please, get it away!"

Elsie tugged Mac a few steps back. He whined and broke away from her, chasing the frog. Jemmie curled into a ball and began to cry.

DiAndreo got to his feet and looked down at the sobbing man in disgust. "Bad move, Demarais. You're under arrest. You have the right to remain silent…" He completed the rest of the recitation and then helped him sit up. "What do we do with you now?" he added sarcastically.

"Pictures?" Sue suggested. She still looked a little pale, but she had recovered well. Elsie looked grim and angry as she called her dog to heel. Enormous gratitude toward them both washed over Tom.

"Pictures, definitely. But not just yet. Let's not mess up the scene by moving around. Stay away from the boggy places if you can, and let's see if we can get some help."

The next half hour wore on as Elsie handed over her cell phone and Tom made the call to 911 to set things in motion. He sent her and Mac back to the road to guide the local police in, while he and Sue guarded Jemmie. The man didn't seem to realize where he was or what he had done; every now and then he shuddered and looked around wild-eyed, as if a plague of frogs might pop into existence and devour him. Tom almost felt sorry for him, except when he panicked and struggled against his bonds. Then he was too busy subduing him to feel any pity.

After one brief outburst, during which Jemmie came close to tossing the cop off him, Tom glared up at Sue. "You could've helped," he panted. "Where were— What are you doing?"

Sue had opened the box and begun to photograph each paper inside it, one by one. She made a neat pile of them on top of the spread-out oilcloth. "Taking pictures," she said without returning his stare. She had a latex glove on one hand.

"You can't do that!" he cried. "That's police evidence—"

"You're the cop, not me. Shut up and keep your

eye on Jemmie. I want to look at these, and I'll never get a chance if I don't do it now."

"Sue, I'm warning you—" He broke off as Jemmie bucked under him. The man seemed to find an extra reserve of manic energy and was much harder to control this time. His belted legs lashed out and connected with the back of Tom's knees. He swayed with the blow, stumbled on a loose root, and went down. They rolled in the mud, scrabbling for a hold. Jemmie squealed and cursed as Tom finally got a knee into his back. He shuddered and lay face down, quivering.

"You gonna behave now? Or do I have to add resisting arrest to your list of violations?" Tom waited a few minutes, then returned his attention to Sue.

By that time, she had taken up a perch on one of the rocks and returned his gaze with no sign she might have done anything illegal. The camera and glove were nowhere in sight. The closed cash box sat beside her. Tom opened his mouth, then shut it with a snap. He'd have it out with her later. To tell the truth, he wanted a look at those photos himself. He'd square it with regulations somehow.

At last Elsie, without the dog, brought the locals down the trail. Two police officers took charge of Jemmie, untying his feet and marching him back to the road. Another, whose nametag proclaimed him to be "Sanger," started to ask questions and make notes. He produced a camera and took a lot of photographs.

The rain started up again, reminding them they were very wet, muddy, and cold. Elsie produced the thermos of hot sweet tea, which helped, but they needed dry clothes and warmth. "I'm taking the women back to their car," Tom told the Douglass officer. His tone said he would brook no argument. The local guy took one look at their blue lips and shooed them off. "Just don't leave without giving us your names," he warned.

"I got it," Tom replied. He led them away.

Mac greeted them with enthusiastic yips and wiggles when they got back to the truck, and they sank into the seats with grateful sighs. The heater worked wonders on their shivering, and before long, they began to shed some of their wet outerwear. Sue pulled some trail bars from her backpack.

"I always keep a couple in there," she explained as they munched eagerly.

Elsie made a neat bundle of her trail bar wrapper and stowed it into a trash bag dangling from the glove box handle. She drained the last of her tea and relaxed back into her seat. "Well," she said in her quiet, dignified way, "I learned something today."

The others looked at her, Tom with surprise, Sue with expectation. "And just what did you learn?" Sue encouraged her friend.

"I learned I'm really not cut out for police work."

Sue melted into helpless giggles as she tried to object. "You? The gun? That frog...I never...Oh!" She dissolved in shouts of nervous laughter before she managed to gain a measure of control. Wiping the tears from her eyes, she gasped, "Where did you ever learn to handle a gun?"

"From Archer Mayor novels." Elsie said it as if it were obvious.

That set Sue off again. This time Tom's booming chuckles joined in. Elsie regarded them with serious concern until the utter silliness infected her, too. The truck rocked with their hilarity.

Tom was grateful they had such a healthy release from tension. He got thrown into situations like this all the time, so he knew how stressful they could be. Getting over the first shakes with a round of laughter was a very sane reaction.

"What I don't understand," Sue began, between hiccups of leftover giggles, "is how Jemmie could have snuck up on us. I'm usually pretty aware of what's going on in the woods, and Elsie has great hearing. She can always tell what truck is pulling up outside our door at work."

Tom jumped in before they could take any blame on themselves. "That's my fault. I had my suspicions— remember the car that splashed us before we walked in? It followed us off the highway. I should have been more careful and kept better watch. Besides, with the rain coming down, it was hard to hear anything else."

"I was listening for Mac," Elsie admitted. "I was worried about him."

"And we were all so intent on digging up the box." Sue satisfied herself with that explanation.

Tom's face grew stern. "Speaking of that box… Sue, you were way out of line taking pictures of it."

She had the grace to look remorseful. "I was careful, Tom. I only handled them by the edges, and I put them back exactly the way they came out. And I had that glove."

"That's not the point," he snapped. "You might have jeopardized the whole case."

Without hesitation, Sue opened a port on her camera and extracted the memory card. "Well, then, here. You keep the pictures. You don't have to tell anyone about them if you don't want to. If the Douglass cops don't get curious about what's in the box, you can use them to nudge your buddies into looking at the case." She shivered as she handed over the tiny gadget. "In case you're wondering, it looked to me like they were all appraisals for jewelry."

Tom shot her a glance of hot anger, but he accepted the memory card. He turned it in his fingers. "I suppose an extra set of photos won't hurt. But dammit, don't you ever do anything like that again!"

Sue looked suitably chastened, but then she grinned. "One thing for sure, though. We found out where that painting was made."

Chapter Nineteen

Ginny was still contemplating the problem of how to identify one particular Rotarian with the minimal information she had dragged out of Matt Baldwin. She must know someone who was active in the Rotary Club and could point her in the right direction. As for Matt's story of a volunteer finding the painting along the side of the road—forget it. That was impossible. Jerry Berger had been quite aware of the value of his work, and he would never have let any of his prints, let alone an original, fall out of a car. If he couldn't deliver it in person, he relied on a trustworthy courier to transport anything that needed transporting.

That started her thinking about Yaneque Duprey and trying to work out how she could be involved, but before she could finish her thought the door opened. She turned to greet the customer who entered and had to choke back a cry.

It wasn't Jerry Berger, of course, only Jerry's younger brother Howard. He looked so much like Jerry, Ginny could have wept. He had the same thick eyebrows and sharp nose. His eyes were just as blue as Jerry's, although Howard's lacked their startling intensity. His hair was trimmed shorter and turning gray. He was a little more inclined to fat than Jerry had been, but perhaps if Jerry had lived, he too would have developed a little softness around the middle. Howard, moreover, had none of his brother's artistic ability or temperament. He was a solid, reliable man nearing fifty, who managed Jerry's estate with conscientious honesty. Ginny respected him but couldn't muster any real warmth for him. "Hi, Howard. I didn't expect to see you so soon."

He fixed himself a cup of coffee and settled down in a chair across the worktable from her. "I had some business in Mill Falls and thought I'd stop in on the way by. Thanks for calling us about the new painting. Can I see it?"

"Of course. Drink your coffee first. Have you found any time to get into the archives?" She couldn't refer to it as "the attic," as Pam called the storage area where all of Jerry's sketches, notes, and papers were kept. Pam, the only sister of Howard and Jerry, was supposed to be going through the boxes of stuff and putting them into some semblance of order, but homeschooling her three children took all her time. In the end, Ginny supposed, she would have to do it herself—someday.

"I did some poking around," Howard told her. "I remembered a box Jerry labeled 'Abby.' It took some hunting for, I'll tell you. You know that little alcove way at the back, where the roof cuts down toward the dormer? It was back in there. I had to clear a path through all the old paint and boxes of paper. Whew! What a mess. I think I'll have to hire a couple of art students next summer and go through it myself. Poor Pam doesn't have the time.

"Anyway, I found the box and I took it downstairs. Pam let me use her back bedroom. I took everything out and sorted it on the bed. There were lots of photos of

Abby, in all kinds of costumes, and some—" He broke off and sucked at his coffee for a long minute. "Do you have a brother?"

"No, just a younger sister. There was a cousin I looked up to, though."

Howard nodded. "It's really hard to think of your big brother all grown up, and then to look back at the bits and pieces that are left of his life. I suppose I always knew that—I mean, Jerry was a man, and a man has his needs. You know what I mean. He took some absolutely stunning photos of Abby. Nothing dirty, nothing like that. But very sexy, very sensual. There were sketches, too, of her and some other woman. At least one other woman, maybe two. It was like he was looking at women for the first time. As an artist, I mean. He would draw just an arm, or the side of a face, or the back. He was getting better and better at it."

Howard frowned and shook his head in perplexity. "Such a damn shame. All this time and I still can't believe he killed himself. I keep asking why, why…why would he do such a thing? He never gave any hint—" His sudden rush of anger ran out of energy and dried up. He shrugged and continued. "There was lots of other stuff in that box, too. Lots of photos of landscapes, especially some rocks in the woods some place. He liked to go out and shoot the same place over and over until he got the light just where he wanted it. This one particular place, he must've shot ten rolls of film. Abby was in some of the pictures, posing. Pretty place."

"You didn't happen to bring along any of those pictures, did you, Howard?" Ginny kept her voice casual and even, with great effort. It was a good thing

143

Howard didn't realize how much pain he was causing her.

"I did, as a matter of fact. We can go out to the house one day soon and look through everything in the box if you think we need to. There was one thing in particular that intrigued me, so I brought it along." He reached into the inside pocket of his jacket and brought out an envelope. He hesitated a moment before he handed it to her.

Ginny looked at it curiously, turning it over once or twice. It looked like an ordinary business envelope, yellowed with age. On the front, in Jerry's florid hand, was written the single word, "Abby."

She was suddenly afraid to open it. "What's in here?" Her voice trembled.

"Not much. Just a receipt from RunAround. Nothing personal. It just didn't seem to belong in that box, so I brought it with me."

Reassured, Ginny opened the envelope and unfolded the yellow duplicate of a standard receipt form. The RunAround logo was printed across the top, with the date written in just below it. The package was described as "painting" with no further detail and valued at $100—a standard minimum value. The pickup location was listed as Jerry's address, and the delivery address was Brush & Bevel.

She looked up at him. "It says here this was picked up ten years ago. That would've been after he started sending his work to Foxwood Editions in Maine for printing. I wasn't handling his prints then. Why would he have been sending me a painting?"

"I don't know," Howard said. "But if the coroner was correct, that date was just about the day he died."

The world turned dark and spun. When Ginny opened her eyes, she was slumped across the arm of the chair with Howard bent over her with deep concern.

"What is it?" Howard exclaimed. "Ginny, are you all right?"

He offered her a sip of his coffee, which she refused, and helped her sit up. "A little water?" she requested.

He hastened to the dispenser, poured a cupful, and set it in her hand. She drank gratefully and felt her trembling ease off. Howard hovered close to her. "Shall I call an ambulance?"

She gave her head a shake and kept her eyes shut against the vertigo. "I'm okay." Hearing how weak she sounded but feeling strength return, she repeated, "I'm okay. Really. I just thought—oh, Howard, what if he was sending me a message? I never got it; I swear I didn't. But it's here. After all this time, it's here."

"What's here, Ginny?" he said, patently not believing her.

"The painting Jerry was trying to send to me. He was trying to tell me something, and I never got the message until too late. Come with me, I'll show you."

He held his hand under her elbow as she led him downstairs and unlocked the safe. By then she was steady again. When she took out the Berger painting and laid it on the table, he leaned over it intently, all but ignoring her. He studied it inch by inch, examined the signature, and then let out a deep breath. His hand went back into his pocket, and he drew out a photograph.

"I found this in the box marked Abby," he said.

It matched the painting perfectly.

Chapter Twenty

The rain had stopped again. The sky was clear over Mount Monadnock to the west as Elsie turned her truck east onto the highway and headed home. She checked to be sure Tom, following in his car, had made the turn, then took a look at the still-dark clouds ahead. The lowering sun cast a red glow on them, but they were breaking up. Sue sat beside her, eyes closed, her head resting against the window.

The Douglass police had let them go when they finished their initial inquiries into the incident in the woods. Elsie wondered how long Tom would let them go on believing Jemmie had interrupted a game of geocaching and become more unhinged than usual. The plan was to take him to the local hospital for observation and treatment. She hoped Tom would be able to clear the air with the Douglass cops without involving her and Sue.

"I hope Tom doesn't get into trouble," Sue worried as the truck descended Temple Pass. She sat up and glanced over her shoulder at Tom's car. "The Douglass cops didn't seem very happy with him."

"I hope you don't get into trouble," Elsie retorted.

"About those pictures? Nah. If Tom finds anything on them, he can ask the Douglass cops to take a look. No need to involve me. What I want to know is...how did Jemmie know where to go today?"

"He's always hanging around downstairs. It would've been easy for him to overhear us deciding to go out to Douglass, but why would he think it had anything to do with him?"

"He was very upset when he saw me cleaning that painting," Sue reminded Elsie.

"But that's no reason to follow us all the way out there. And on such a miserable day."

"Well, I'm just glad you had Mac with us. Things could have been a lot worse if he hadn't showed up when he did."

Elsie was embarrassed but pleased. "He's such a goofball. Off chasing frogs."

"But it was brilliant of him to put one in Jemmie's hand. Good thing the bullet went wide and didn't hit anyone. I wonder if the police found it."

"I doubt they even looked for it," Elsie decided, after they spent some time thinking about everything. "Since no one was hurt there wasn't any reason to search. You were great, swinging that stick of yours! Remind me never to make you mad."

"And you, holding that gun. Would you have shot it if Tom couldn't bring Jemmie down?"

Elsie downshifted and slowed to go around a car parked on the side of the road, gathering up the road-cleaning volunteers. "I don't know," she said soberly as she resumed speed. "Maybe if he was coming at me I could. Or at you. I think it would have to happen so fast I couldn't think about it."

"Mmmm," Sue sank back into the seat and relaxed. "It's over and I'm glad. I hope they keep Jemmie in the hospital for a long time."

The sky cleared up as they drove east. Elsie's

spirits rose as the light brightened, but she still felt very tired, more from the danger than from the physical exertion. Mac, too, was tuckered out, resting on the old blanket in his crate in the back of the truck. Elsie dropped him off at home, then drove in companionable silence with Sue back to Brush & Bevel, where they had agreed to meet up with Tom again and fill Ginny in on their adventure.

****

Howard Berger was still at the gallery when they arrived. Sue was struck by how much he resembled his brother. She thought it was a very good thing that Jemmie, in his present condition, wasn't around to see him. Ginny looked upset and tired. She seemed surprised to see them, but took one long look at them and flipped the door sign around to read "Closed."

"You're a mess! Did you have fun?"

They looked at each other and burst out laughing. "Yes and no," Sue told her, and launched into a recap of their day. Ginny was horrified.

"I should never have let you go!" she cried when Sue, supplemented by Elsie, had finished telling the story.

"Like you could have stopped us. We're grownups. We had a dog and a policeman with us. Anyway, we're fine, and we found out where the nude was painted. I bet you haven't had such a productive day."

It was Ginny's turn to laugh. "I think I have, in my own way. I didn't get shot at, but I did find out more about where the painting has been for the past ten years. Howard found a picture in Jerry's effects that proves he was planning to do it. So it's been a good day all around." She filled in the details, except for the amount she was sending to Matt Baldwin. They exclaimed over their good luck. "I still don't know how it got from RunAround, if Yaneque did pick it up, to the guy who left it at the bar. I don't think I believe that story about picking it up off the side of the road."

The image of the road crew flashed into Sue's mind. "I'm not so sure. There were volunteers cleaning up the road today, and I remember seeing a Rotary sign—you know the ones that say 'this road has been adopted by such and such a group'? I'm pretty sure the Rotary does that section of the highway."

"But how would the painting have gotten there?" Ginny objected.

"Isn't that when Yaneque had her accident? If the car was totaled, maybe everything that was in it got lost at the same time. Then when the Rotary came around to pick it up, somebody found the picture and kept it." Sue gave a shrug, belying her excitement in her theory.

"I'll check it out," Tom volunteered, to their surprise. He'd been quiet so far, content to listen to their reports to each other. They weren't trained at conveying complex information, but they'd done a good job.

But Ginny shook her head. "Thanks, but I'll follow it up myself. Unless it has something to do with the police end of it? I'll call and see if anyone remembers picking up anything unusual. It would be very interesting for the background story if it turns out we can publish prints."

Tom agreed. "It looks to me like you've pretty much established your—what did you call it? Provenance?" He ticked off his points on his fingers. "The pictures Mr. Berger brought in indicate Jerry intended to paint the picture and did paint it. We've shown we can find the place. There's the receipt for transport, the story about finding it by the road, and a pretty good trail once it gets to the bar. If you can trace it to the Rotary, will you need anything else?" He gave Ginny a moment to think about it, and continued when she shook her head. "Fine. I still need a lot of information, which I'm hoping you can give me. What do you know about Mike Bingham?"

"Mike?" Ginny repeated in surprise. "Very little. He was only in here once or twice, always with Abby, except for the time, you know, when he threatened Elsie. After Abby died he moved out west, I think. Sold the insurance agency and resigned as alderman—"

"Oh, good heavens!" Sue interrupted her. "That clump of bushes where we found the box, that was swamp alder! Do you think he chose that on purpose?"

"Who? Jerry? What do you mean?" Tom asked.

Sue waved her hand to indicate she needed to think. "Mike Bingham was an alderman in Mill Falls, right? And in the picture, Abby was pointing at the alder. With blood dripping out of her hand. Do you think that was a clue, that whatever is in the box has something to do with the 'alder-man'? Something about his position?" She frowned at her theory. "It sounds crazy, but I wonder if Jerry was afraid *Mike* was going to kill him and Abby. Were they having an affair?" she asked Ginny and Howard. "Was Mike the kind of guy who would be so jealous he'd kill?"

Howard shook his head. "I never thought Jerry killed himself. It just wasn't like him, but an affair is a different matter. He liked the ladies. I don't know about Mike, though. I never knew him."

Elsie stirred, but before she could comment, Tom DiAndreo put his oar in. "Wait, I want to go back a minute. I think Sue might have a good idea there, that what is in the box might have something to do with Mike's position as alderman. There was something around that time going on in Mill Falls about tax irregularities… Damn, I can't remember. I'll look it up back at the office. It's probably nothing. But why would there be appraisals from Jemmie's if it had to do with Mike as an alderman?"

"I still think Jemmie did it," Elsie insisted. "He's crazy enough to do it. Maybe Jerry and Abby found out something about Jemmie, and that's why the appraisals are in there. The alder bush is just a coincidence."

Sue deflated. "You're probably right. Alder is everywhere in boggy places like that. If it were witch hazel, I'd be looking for a coven."

"Well, what sort of motive might Jemmie have, if he were the killer?" Tom continued. "Assuming it really was a double murder and not murder/suicide as they determined ten years ago."

Several voices rose at once, denying the suicide.

"Jerry didn't own a gun!"

"Have you seen *One Year*?"

"No way he would have killed himself. Everything was just starting for him as an artist!"

Tom made soothing motions with his hands. "I'm assuming somebody else killed them, okay? Let's assume it was Jemmie. Why would he do it?"

"Because he was nuts," Elsie declared. "You know how he is."

Sue chuckled. "Yeah, maybe Abby wanted him to make her a frog brooch." That provoked a round of laughter. Even Tom joined in.

"Okay," he went on after they calmed down, "just because Jemmie was nuts. Maybe she insulted him, or maybe he just fixated on her—we'll never know. How about this...what if he cheated her on the jewelry and she found out? How would she have known? But then," he muttered, half to himself, "why would she confide in Jerry and not her husband, or the police?" He put his chin in his hand, deep in thought. "We need more information. Leave it to me. I have resources you don't. Besides, you've already put yourselves in danger. I'm serious, folks. Don't do anything without running it by me, understand?"

"But Jemmie's under arrest," Ginny objected.

"We have no idea if someone else was involved. Even that guy you talked to about the painting, that bar owner, might know more than we think he might."

"You're getting married next week, right?" Elsie asked.

He blinked at the change of subject, but he couldn't prevent the happy smile that lit up his rather dark features. "Yeah. I'll be away for a week on our honeymoon—"

"Where are you going?"

"Cancun. We've gone down there a couple of times and we love it. The scuba and snorkeling is out of this world. Anyway, don't worry. Jemmie is going to be held for at least a week in the hospital, until he's stabilized. They'll keep him longer if they think he's a danger to himself or others. In the meantime, I'll do some checking around, talk to some contacts here and there. You folks just sit tight and do your jobs. Let me do mine. Okay?"

"I want to call the Rotary Club in Churchville or Douglass to see if anyone there picked up the painting," Ginny insisted.

Tom thought for a moment. "I can't see any harm in that. But anything else, talk to me first, okay?"

Sue hesitated. "About those photos?"

"I never saw you take any photos."

"Oh." She bit her lip. She'd never seen his eyes look so stony.

He relented a bit. "I'll let you know what I can. I have to talk to Douglass and the Major Crimes Unit."

He'd better act fast, he thought, before Elsie took that dog for another walk.

Chapter Twenty-One

Two days later, Jenna Rudolph was back in Brush & Bevel to view her cleaned painting. Ginny fetched it from the safe and set in her hands. She held it up to the light and admired it from several angles, tilting her head this way and that. "It really cleaned up beautifully. I like it much better now. It was so dark and dim. And you're sure this is a real Jerry Berger?"

"Yes," Ginny assured her. "I've compared the signature to quite a few others we have on record. On his other paintings and on things like checks, as well. His artistic signature was rather distinctive. Here, I'll show you."

Ginny had prepared this little demonstration with care. She had an assortment of Jerry's prints ready to display to Jenna. "Here, you can see how he signed the original of *A Walk in the Rain*, and in the margin here he countersigned it in pencil. That's the normal thing for a limited edition print, you know. The pencil signature looks different, of course, because a pencil is easier to write with than a paintbrush. You can see the same thing on these other prints." She pointed them out to Jenna, letting the woman take her time to examine them.

Jenna looked them over, comparing one to another, and all of them to the name on the lower right corner of the nude. She chewed her lip for a moment. "To my eye they look the same. You would know best, since you are familiar with his work. You say you've found evidence in his studio papers that he was working on this?"

Ginny brought out the photograph Howard had discovered. "My staff have also found the location of the rocks," she added, without revealing the aftermath of that ill-advised venture. "So if you're asking if I'm sure this is a Jerry Berger, the answer is yes, I'm sure. I have absolutely no doubt this is a previously unknown work by him."

Jenna sat back in her chair and held the painting up before her. "It really is beautiful," she repeated, her earlier reserve vanishing. "That woman is so pretty, and the light... The light is just perfect. What about this line of red drops? Do you know what that's about?" Her finger traced the line of red from Abby's hand, down the rocks, and into the alder bush.

"We don't know," Ginny lied, touching her finger to her nose. "Maybe it had some significance to them, or just to Jerry." She broke off and shrugged. "Maybe it will always be a mystery."

The other woman accepted that without a quibble. "I suppose the next question would be...how much is this worth? How do you figure that out?"

"It's a very subjective process," Ginny began, relieved Jenna hadn't pursued the meaning of the red drops. "I compared it to other post mortem works by recent artists who died suddenly—there aren't many of Jerry's caliber—and I made some adjustments I think are in line with the prices his other originals are going for, as far as I can tell."

"What do you mean, as far as you can tell?"

"There is no way to know if the paintings have gone in private sales, from one collector to another. That happens all the time. Unless I contact the first owner and track down all the subsequent ones, I don't know who they are or what they paid. Most likely, they wouldn't be willing to disclose what they paid. Jerry completed only one other painting of a nude that I know of, and this one is much, much better. All in all, I would be very surprised if this one sold for less than twenty-five thousand."

Jenna gasped. "That much? But I only paid seventy-five dollars for it!"

"You got lucky," Ginny reminded her.

They went on to discuss the details of a potential sale agreement. Ginny, of course, would take a cut for her work as agent. There would be further fees if Jenna agreed to allow prints to be made. Still, the Rudolphs stood to gain the bulk of any money generated by this painting.

"Would the estate take a cut as well?"

Ginny considered that for a moment. "You know, I'd have to check that out. I'd have to read the terms of the will again to see if this picture would be included in the bequest." When Jenna seemed about to object, Ginny hastened to add, "Oh, there's no doubt you own it now. I'd have to check with a lawyer, of course, but I think Pam and Howard would come to terms without much fuss. If, for instance, you were to offer them a percentage of the sale, if you sold it, or of the print income if you decide to go that route."

Jenna looked at the picture and gave a rueful little laugh. "All I wanted was to get this thing cleaned up in time for my husband's birthday. I never imagined I was getting into so much hot water!"

You don't know the half of it. Once again she held her tongue.

"Well," Jenna went on in a brisk voice, "what do I owe you for cleaning this? And shall we see about framing it?"

"We can include the cleaning in the frame price, if you like. Let's see, this needs a big frame."

Ginny asked Jenna about the room where the picture would hang. Were there other paintings? What were the furnishings like? What color were the wall and the upholstery? Did Jenna and Bob have any preferences in framing? Did they prefer gold or wood, simple or carved, classic or modern? Armed with the answers, Ginny selected half a dozen frame samples to start, explaining that the frame needed to be deep enough to cover the stretcher bars.

"Speaking of the stretcher bars," she added, "these are not in the best shape. They've gotten warped and there seems to be some mold in them. It really would be best if we put it on new stretchers with all the proper conservation techniques."

"What do you mean?" Jenna asked.

"It's best if the canvas never actually touches the wood. Wood is acidic, and that can make the canvas brittle. Don't worry, we can deal with it and do it all the time. We'll seal the stretchers so no acid can get to the canvas. When we put it in the frame, we'll make sure the painting is buffered from that wood as well. With a valuable painting like this, it's worth the extra care."

Jenna agreed and they spent another half an hour selecting a frame. In the end, she chose a wide gold frame with simple beading along the inner edge and rich red tones in the gilding. She gulped a little at the price, but the frame did enhance the painting. She was wavering when another customer walked in the front door, took one look at the picture as it lay on the design table with the frame sample on one corner, and gave a heartfelt, "Wow! That looks terrific."

Jenna looked up in surprise, and Ginny laughed. "I couldn't have planned that! Jenna, this is our friend Martin. He's been a customer of ours for years. He has excellent taste."

"Ginny has taught me a lot," Martin added. "I trust her completely."

"In that case, I'll go with it. You're right, it looks very good."

"Wait 'til you see it finished. You'll love it." Ginny called Elsie upstairs to deal with the work Martin was picking up, and then she finished pricing Jenna's work. "It will take two to three weeks."

Jenna hesitated. "Oh. Should I have it insured in the meantime? I don't mean to imply…"

Ginny was not insulted. "Oh, I carry a lot of insurance. Don't worry about that. A piece like this we store in what we call the safe, a walk-in closet with its own security code. We've never lost any artwork, and we'll take extra special care with this one, believe me. Once it's done, we can talk about having an unveiling, if you like. Whether or not you want to sell it, it would be a good way to introduce it to the world."

"Maybe that would help us determine the value?" Jenna had adjusted in a hurry to the idea of owning very expensive art.

"Yes, that, too. Then you could insure it for as much as necessary."

"Thank you, for everything, Ginny. You've been wonderful."

"My pleasure, Jenna," Ginny replied, but she was weeping inside. She had done it all for Jerry.

Chapter Twenty-Two

Sue had decided to sacrifice another precious day off to her curiosity. She was back at the offices of the *Town Crier,* chasing down that story on the tax irregularities in Mill Falls. Jim, the reporter, had met her again, teasing her about becoming a private eye.

Sue teased him back. "It could be worse. Maybe I'll become a reporter and take your job away from you!"

Jim groaned. "You wouldn't want it. Meetings about zoning changes—dull, duller, and dullest. Last night I sat around for two hours while the Harpersville Zoning Board of Adjustment talked about driveways, for God's sake. Now I gotta go interview builders who will, to a man—well, two men and one woman—absolutely hate the new regs. What are you looking up?"

"That same old business about the Berger-Bingham murders. I just need to nail down some dates. Hey, is there a way to make copies of the pages I need?"

Jim showed her how to do that and then took his leave, wearing a melodramatic look of martyrdom. "What I don't do for the press!"

Sue found the microfiche she wanted, but she skipped over the reports on Jerry and Abby. She checked her memories of Yaneque's accident, then went on to the brief article about the improper auto registrations and the tax problems it was causing for Douglass. It was a little puzzling. It seemed a number of cars and trucks that should have been registered in Mill Falls had been registered in Douglass instead. The taxes on those cars had then been paid to Douglass rather than to Mill Falls. Once the problem was discovered, the city of Mill Falls pressured Douglass to return the funds, but Douglass had already spent the money. At the time of the story, Douglass was trying to figure out how they could repay the money they were not entitled to without busting their town budget. According to the newspaper reports, angry letters flew between the lawyers for the two towns.

Sue sat back and thought about it all. How had the improper registration occurred in the first place? Normally, a car owner showed up at town hall in whatever town he or she lived in, registered the car, and paid the taxes. In small towns where everyone knew everyone else, there was no need to verify the addresses given on the registration forms. Sometimes, however, people mailed the forms in, especially when they were renewing the registration. Ah, she thought, that's how it happened. But why would anyone bother to register a car in one town when they lived in another? The taxes were the same all over the state.

One thing varied among the towns in New Hampshire. Sue took a break from the dingy archives in the basement and made a quick telephone call. Sure enough, insurance was a lot more expensive in Mill Falls than it was in Douglass. She wondered if other small towns had experienced a rash of wrong registrations. And then she had another thought:

Mike Bingham had owned an insurance agency.

Chapter Twenty-Three

While Sue was in Douglass and Ginny was upstairs with Jenna, Elsie worked downstairs to log in the weekend's new work orders that would be processed in the next two weeks. The precision measuring and double-checking were soothing to her roiled nerves. By noon, she had set up the work to be done on ten pieces, ordered the mats and frames as needed, and made notes on any questions that arose.

Elsie had just finished up the last piece, a double matted arrangement of five openings for old family photos, when she heard a knock on the door followed immediately by Yaneque's entrance. The courier carried a plastic zipper-top bag with a dozen or so assorted buttons in it. Another advantage of using RunAround was Yaneque's less stringent packaging requirement compared to other delivery services, although she could be strict when it came to fragile or valuable items.

"I've delivered some strange things in this job," she said as she came in, "but this takes the cake. What the heck are you planning to do with these?"

Taking the bag with a chuckle, Elsie signed the delivery receipt and pulled an empty frame, some old-fashioned wire-rim glasses, and a rusty pair of scissors out of the storage area. Without a word, she put them on the table, took the buttons out of the bag, and set them into place along with the scissors and glasses. Yaneque drew a deep breath.

"Oh, wow," she marveled. "Are those real antique buttons?"

Elsie picked one or two up. "Some of them are. I think these are ivory. The scissors came from a yard sale, but they look neat, don't they? I think we're still waiting for a bit of crocheted lace before we finish this piece."

"That's beautiful. I never would've thought of doing that."

They chatted a bit, comparing notes about the weather and their respective businesses. Yaneque asked about Maculato's training and Elsie asked if another PT Cruiser was in the cards yet. Yaneque was almost ready to leave when Elsie said, as if it didn't matter, "I've been meaning to ask you…that day you had your accident, was it snowing when you got to Jerry Berger's place?"

"No, it was just changing over," Yaneque began. She stared at Elsie. "I—how did I remember that? I haven't been able to recall anything after leaving my house that day!"

"What else do you remember?" Elsie asked, again without any pressure. "What was his road like?"

"It was muddy and potholed. This is great! I can see it now. I remember turning onto his road—he lived back in the boonies, you know. It was cold and there was snow in the air. Jerry was waiting for me outside."

"Did you see any other car there?"

"No. Just him, standing there with a package in his hand. He was really nervous about something. He didn't want to chat like he usually did. I gave him his receipt and I said something about why he had to live back of beyond, and then—" she faltered. "I don't remember anything else. Geez, Elsie, how did you do that? Even when I was in rehab I couldn't remember that much."

Elsie shrugged. "It's a trick I learned when my mom was losing her memory. Sometimes if I asked something very specific, she could remember it. It didn't always work."

Yaneque tilted her head and tapped her finger against her lips. "They told me my memory might come back some day, in bits and pieces. They said it might take a long time, too, or it might never happen. What made you think of it?"

Elsie touched her finger to her nose. "Thinking about my mother. I hope it doesn't bring up bad memories for you. It must have been awful."

"It probably was, but I don't remember. Even now, I don't remember any more of it. Just that little bit, like a scene in a snow globe. Thank you! I'll call up my doctor and see if we can go any further with it. I hate having this big hole in my mind."

"I'm glad you aren't upset. I wouldn't want you to be mad at me."

"Oh, no! I'm so happy you asked. It means that part of my mind is healing. I've always been worried I might've done something really stupid and forgotten it." She giggled.

Yaneque bounced out the door, looking considerably relieved. Elsie felt as if she had played a dirty trick on the courier. Despite Yaneque's gratitude, she was displeased with herself. But she had gleaned one shred of information; Abby Bingham wasn't at

Jerry Berger's when Yaneque arrived there.

****

Upstairs, now that Jenna had gone home, Ginny was on the phone. She seemed to spend half her working life on the phone these days. There was one more gap to fill in before she could feel confident about the provenance of the Berger. Even though she was sure of her identification, if Matt Baldwin's wild tale about the Rotarian was correct, it would add a wonderful bit of color to the history of the piece. As if the deaths of the painter and his model needed any embellishment.

She had, after half a dozen phone calls, determined which local Rotary conducted road cleanups on Temple Pass and coaxed the name of the club president out of the Churchville town clerk. Ginny was now waiting for the man to pick up his phone and wondering how she was going to approach him.

"Hello?"

"Is this Jeff Jasper?"

"Uh-huh."

"Mr. Jasper, my name is Ginny Brent. I'm a freelance writer, and I'm doing a story on the different adopt-a-highway groups in southern New Hampshire." She rubbed her nose at the glibness of her lie. "Do you have a few minutes to talk to me?"

He swallowed the bait, eager to get publicity for his group. "Sure. We've been doing that for ten or twelve years now."

"You do the section of highway that runs over Temple Pass, don't you?"

"Uh-huh. Let me tell you, it gets real messed up with all the traffic through there."

"How often do you do the clean up?"

"Twice a year, spring and fall. Soon after the snow melts and then again in October after the leaf peepers go away. You know how they love to get up on Pack Monadnock there? Well, you wouldn't believe the trash they throw out of their cars. Them and the truckers."

"What sort of things do you find along the road?"

"Mostly food wrappers, beer cans, coffee cups. Water bottles, that sort of thing."

"How about car parts, tires?"

"Uh-huh, some of that. Windshield wipers. I never had a windshield wiper come off my car, but I guess it happens. We find a lot of them. The mud flaps from trucks, they come off a lot, too. A tailpipe now and then. Once we found a whole brake rotor, must've been from an accident."

"Do you go up there yourself, Mr. Jasper? How many members work on the crew?"

"Well, we try to get as many as we can, you know. Members, spouses, kids. A lot depends on the weather. If it's a decent day, more people come. If it's real hot or real cold, or if it's raining, not so many. I'd say at least ten each time, sometimes more. We buy subs and drinks and have a little picnic there at the park afterward."

"It sounds like fun."

"Yeah, it is. I mean, it's hard work, but we make it fun. See who can bag the most stuff, or find the weirdest things."

Good, this was heading the way she wanted to go. "What's the weirdest thing you ever found? You personally or someone else in the group?"

"Hmm. Set of falsies once. One of those stuffed deer heads—you know what I mean? The trophy to hang on the wall? Yeah, I think we found two of them one year. Couple times we found eyeglasses, donated them to the Lion's Club. Oh, and one year one of the guys claimed he found a painting."

"A painting?" Ginny put a world of doubt into her voice to cover her excitement. "One of those velvet Elvis things?"

"No, I think it was a nude. Some br—" He stopped and censored himself. "A naked lady in the woods. I never saw it, but everybody talks about it."

"Gee, I'd really like to talk to the man who found that," Ginny encouraged him. "Would it be in the club records someplace? Do you keep a list of who worked on that project and some of the things they found?"

"I can find out for you," Jasper offered. "What paper did you say you work for?"

After eliciting his promise to call her back with the name and phone number of the Rotarian who had found what she was sure was the Berger, Ginny left the garrulous old man with the impression she was going to submit an article to several of the local and regional magazines. *Maybe I could write and submit something.* She patted her nose. Maybe it wasn't a lie.

Chapter Twenty-Four

The Chowdah Bowl was busier than ever this evening. Sue stood in line at the counter about two weeks after the adventure in the woods. Every table was full. Servers bustled between the dining room and the kitchen as if on roller skates. There was a pleasant rumble of conversation punctuated by the clink of spoons in crockery and the rattle of ice-filled glasses.

She stretched her back and shifted from one foot to another. After a long day at work, she was tired and looking forward to a hot meal. Half a dozen customers still stood between her and the take-out counter, even though Ginny had called in her order early in the afternoon. As Brush & Bevel prepared for the unveiling of Jerry's painting, the staff planned to go through the details after hours, over bowls of Mark Horner's good chowder. Sue hoped the meeting wouldn't run too late.

"Hi there," said a voice in her ear.

She turned to find one of Jemmie's erstwhile employees queuing up behind her. "Hi, Sandy. How are things going?" She stifled her guilty feeling. If she and Elsie had just left well enough alone, Sandy and her coworkers would still have jobs. As it was, with Jemmie still held in the hospital, his shop was nearly defunct. The staff was taking care of the repairs and orders he'd left unfinished, but they could take in no new work. Jemmie might be a mental junkyard, but he was an inspired jeweler; no one could take his place. It didn't look like the business would survive without him.

"As well as can be expected," Sandy replied. "We have about another week's worth of stuff to catch up on, and then we're done."

They shuffled forward a step or two. "What happens next?" Sue asked.

Sandy shrugged. "I guess somebody will take over. Jemmie must have had a partner or somebody who will have to oversee the mess. I can't see him coming back any time soon. Besides, his reputation is shot." She rolled her eyes at the pun.

"I feel bad about that. It's sort of my fault—"

"Oh, don't worry about it. Bob and Karen both have new jobs lined up already, and I have a couple of interviews. In a way, it's kind of a relief. Jemmie's been so weird lately."

They stepped aside to allow a heavily-laden server to pass by. "Weirder than usual?" Sue asked. "Ever since I put up that poster with all the frogs?"

Sandy chuckled. "Oh, way before then. He was actually pretty good for a long time, and then about two weeks before the poster, he started freaking out again."

"Do you know, I actually found out there is a kind of frog that has a tooth when it's a tadpole? Just one tooth. It's a desert toad, and it uses the tooth to cannibalize other tadpoles. Weird."

Sandy shuddered. "Please don't ever tell Jemmie. He'd never get over it."

"I can't imagine being so scared of something like a frog, or bugs, or even spiders. Most of them can't hurt us. Was he always afraid of frogs?"

"As long as I've known him." Sandy thought about it for a moment as the line shuffled forward another couple of steps. "Mind you, the frog thing sort of came and went, but he was always worried about bugs and such. He used to be really paranoid about frogs when I first started working here, but then it got a little better. He worried about them, but he only started panicking about them again a few months ago."

Sue laughed. "As long as I can remember, he's been coming downstairs to check on whether frogs were chewing on his storage room door. But you're right, come to think of it—the frog thing only got bad last fall. I wonder what set him off."

Sandy shrugged. "The mind is a mysterious thing. Who knows? I must say, though, as bad as his fear of critters was, he really only freaked out about frogs."

"Poor guy," Sue said, without any deep sympathy. "I hope he can get some help."

"I suppose. It's too late for his business, though." She thought for a moment. "You know what? I think he really lost it a couple of days before he ended up in the hospital."

Sue's ears perked up. "Really? What set him off?"

"I don't know. I gave him this phone message, see, and he just went bonkers. Didn't you hear him?"

"Was that the day Tom DiAndreo talked to him?" They shuffled forward again as another customer collected his order.

"Yeah, I think so. Yes, that's right, we were getting ready to walk out when Tom came in and took charge of him."

Sue chewed her lip. "Do you remember the message?"

"It was just something like, 'go ahead with what we discussed' or something like that."

"Who was it?"

"That's just it, I don't know. It was a guy. I asked his name and he just said, 'He'll know.' So I told Jemmie and he started swearing." Sandy shrugged. "Oh well, I guess we'll never know."

Sue heard her number shouted out. "Well, good luck," she told Sandy as she stepped up to the counter. "That's me," she said to the girl at the register. "Three bowls of chowder."

She agreed to the bread and oyster crackers that came with the chowder and paid the bill. As she headed back to Brush & Bevel, her mind struggled to correlate dates. What could have happened last fall to re-ignite Jemmie's terror of frogs? As far as she could recall, there hadn't been any of the little creatures anywhere near the shop or the mill. Male frogs made a lot of noise in the spring as they tried to impress their ladies, but the mating season would have been long past. Besides, not even the vociferous spring peepers could make themselves heard over the rushing of the river on the other side of the park. Jemmie's reawakened fear must have had some other cause.

Elsie and Ginny greeted her return with hungry appreciation, and for a while, there was only the occasional slurp or contented sigh. Ginny crumbled her crackers into her chowder, while Elsie floated them whole. Sue winnowed out the chunks of clam and set them aside. "I love the chowder," she explained at Ginny's raised eyebrows. "I just don't like all the chewing."

"I just sort of swallow them whole," Elsie said.

"They are rather tough." She scraped the bottom of her bowl with a spoon and then wiped up the last few drops with a chunk of bread. She sighed with contentment. "Mark sure does make real good chowdah."

"Okay, to business." Ginny pushed aside her bowl. Her fingers toyed with the remains of her bread as she passed out lists of things to be done before the unveiling. "Look this over and see what you think."

"Whoa!" Sue exclaimed, looking at the tasks listed under "Publicity." "Who gets to call the Boston TV station?"

"I'll take care of that," Ginny said. "You two are in charge of decorating the shop. I'll want flowers, nice big bouquets. Elsie, can you borrow those red velvet rope things from your church again?"

"They're renting them out now, especially for a commercial event."

"Fine. And a couple of pillars for the flowers, okay? I'll leave it up to your good taste. Just check with me about prices. Sue, will you take charge of doing another banner like we did for our last artist show? And talk to the janitor about lights like he did then, too. They were nice."

"How about some natural items, Ginny?" Elsie suggested. "Maybe some birch saplings in big pots or something like that, to suggest a forest?"

She considered it. "Let's think about that. We'll need lots of room so I don't want to take up floor space with decorations. Oh, how about some sprays for the mantel and such? You could use branches and ferns for that."

Elsie nodded, thinking. "We can put some things together, I think. Maybe even find some trilliums in the woods."

"Trilliums are endangered," Sue objected. "You're not supposed to pick them. We could use lilacs, though. And what about food?"

"The Chowdah Bowl will cater, as usual, and I'll get the wine. Or how about champagne? It's such a special event."

They were discussing the menu when someone rapped on the door. Ginny looked up in annoyance. With all the lights off except for the ones over her desk, none of them had expected any interruptions. Sue really hoped to finish up the meeting early.

The rapping continued. The three women looked at each other, their tension unvoiced. "Shall I get it?" Elsie suggested.

A muffled voice came from outside. "Sue, are you in there? Come on, I see your car here. Sue?"

She got to her feet and peered around the room divider that provided some privacy to Ginny's desk. "It's Tom DiAndreo," she said. "I'd better let him in."

He burst in as soon as she unlocked the door, waving a packet of photos at her. "Have you told anyone about this? Anyone at all?"

"And good evening to you," she replied calmly, although her voice betrayed her quickening heart rate. "Come on back here to the desk. And no, I haven't told a soul, I promise."

He lowered the envelope and followed close on her heels, crowding her. "No one, Sue? It's critical. No boyfriend or girlfriend, even?"

"I haven't even told my cat, and she died three years ago. I may be impulsive, but I'm not stupid. I could see what those things were. Here, sit down and have a soda. By the way, welcome home."

He plopped into the chair she pushed forward for him, staring at her. "Do you realize what you've done? Do you know what's in this package? You could get me in so much trouble—hell, *you* could be in so much trouble!"

Ginny stood up for her employee. "She has answered your question, Tom, so must you harangue her? Now, calm down and tell us all about it. Oh, and wasn't today your swearing in with the state police? Congratulations."

"How was Cancun?" Elsie added. "Did you and Donna have a good time?"

He looked nonplussed at their united front. "Thanks," he said, reluctant to let go of his urgency. "Cancun was great, and I did get sworn in this afternoon. She didn't tell you anything about this?" He waggled the package at them.

"Not a word," Ginny assured him. "What's in there?"

Tom passed a hand over his eyes and swallowed some of the soda. "Motive for murder, I think." He let their stunned faces confirm their ignorance of the envelope's contents. Sue sat still, sure of herself, while Ginny and Elsie exclaimed over his terse comment. He let them get over the first shock. "I was cleaning out my desk at the Westford cop shop this evening. I printed out these photos from her camera. Then I found the newspaper articles she sent me." His face flushed and he wagged a finger at her. "In the first place, you had no business taking the pictures you did, pictures of the contents of the box we all found in the woods that day Jemmie followed us. It could be considered tampering with evidence. The only thing saving you is that the Douglass police force doesn't know you did it."

"I didn't tamper with anything," Sue objected. "I took the pictures and put everything back in the same order. Nothing got lost or changed. The Douglass police have all of it. Not my fault if they haven't followed up."

He glared at her, but she had a point. "All right, so she took the pictures. If I hadn't been away on leave, I would've talked to Douglass anyway. But not only that, she went nosing around in the newspaper files and copied some of them, too."

"Newspapers are open to anyone who asks. I asked. All I did was send you copies of the articles. Besides, I paid for the copies."

Ginny forestalled Tom's retort. "So what did she take pictures of, Tom?"

He sighed. "Appraisals. I'd have to get a jeweler to look at them, but they seem to describe jewelry made for Abby Bingham by Jemmie Demarais."

"Well, we all know he made things for her," Elsie said. "What's the big deal?"

"There are also appraisals of the same items, signed by another jeweler. Thing is, there is a big difference in value from the appraisals Jemmie gave her."

They digested that for a minute. Ginny voiced the obvious conclusion. "He cheated her."

"It appears so."

"And she found out."

"Uh-huh."

"Uh-oh."

"Uh-oh, indeed." Tom leaned forward to emphasize his next point. "There is nothing to prove he cheated her. She could have been the one who got the diamonds replaced by zircons—which is what the appraisals show. Jemmie's papers say there were diamonds, and the other appraisals say they're zircons. Anyway, she could have been setting up a switch on Jemmie for all we know."

"But how would that benefit her?" Elsie asked.

Sue shrugged. "If she could 'prove' he cheated her, even if he hadn't, she could have gotten money out of him. Or other things."

"But that would mean…she would've had to have another jeweler in on the scam," Ginny mused. "That's getting pretty complicated, isn't it?"

Tom nodded. "Here's one scenario…Abby wants money for something or other, maybe for a divorce or to give to Berger. She can't get it from her husband, so she resorts to this scheme to blackmail Jemmie. But it backfires when he refuses to pay and he kills her and the artist, too."

Ginny and Elsie both protested. "She wouldn't do anything like that. She was *nice*, Tom."

"People can be really devious."

"Jerry wasn't," Ginny said. "I knew him well. He was the least devious man I ever met. Besides, Jerry didn't need money. He was doing great."

"Maybe so. That's one scenario. Here's another…Abby paid for diamonds but got zircons. She got suspicious for some reason and confronted him or threatened him with the evidence. Bang, she's dead."

"But why kill Jerry, too?"

Tom shrugged. "He was in the wrong place at the wrong time. Or Jemmie knew about their affair and arranged it to look like a murder/suicide. If so, he did it well, and I'm not sure he would've been capable of it. There is another possibility, though." He looked at Sue.

She squirmed in her chair. "When I was at the newspaper a few weeks ago reading the files about Jerry and Abby, I ran across an article about motor vehicle registrations in Douglass. It just caught my eye as I was scrolling through the microfiches, but when I thought about it later, after we found the box, it bugged me. I checked a few things out, and it looked to me like someone was monkeying around with insurance somehow. I did a little more checking, but then I got scared and left it all for Tom when he got back."

"Probably the smartest thing you've done all spring. I told you, this stuff is best left to the professionals. But Sue was right. Someone was trying to get their company vehicles insured at a lower rate by registering them in a town that has a lower risk. I did a little research myself before I came over here, and it turns out the company did their insurance business with Mike Bingham."

He let them think about it for a while. Sue caught his eye and raised her eyebrow in question. He nodded. She bit her lip.

"But I don't see," Elsie began. "What does that have to do with Abby's jewelry? And anyway, Mike was so upset about her dying he—well, you know. He came in here and threatened me."

"That's why I got scared, Elsie," Sue said. "I think Mike was overcharging this company—it was a construction company—for their insurance and pocketing the extra fees. Then I think he got Jemmie to make diamond jewelry to launder the money. What if Abby found out about it? And then she found out

Jemmie wasn't using diamonds?"

Sue glanced at Tom, who nodded for her to continue. "It gets worse. I started thinking how he could maximize his winnings, so to speak, and I thought...what if he forced Jemmie to use fake diamonds? And then later on, he might stage a theft of the fake jewelry and claim insurance for the real thing. He could make a lot of money that way."

"But if Jemmie went to the police," Elsie objected.

"I think Mike would have threatened him with frogs." Sue chuckled, but she wasn't joking.

Ginny frowned. "Now, really. Okay, so he's afraid of frogs, but I just don't believe that would have kept him from protecting himself from Mike, and I can't imagine Mike doing that anyway."

"You didn't see him in the woods," Elsie told her. "He was doing all right until Mac put the frog in his hand. Then he went absolutely bonkers. Like his mind just snapped." She hesitated. "I can imagine Mike doing something like that. After all, I saw him here, remember." She shivered at the memory.

"He was crazy with grief," Ginny protested.

"Well, maybe he's crazy with greed, too," Sue replied.

Tom jumped back into the conversation. "One of the things I plan to do is call out to Montana and see if there's been any jewelry thefts since Mike moved out there. But—"

There was a shattering crack and the crash of glass exploding. Tom leaped up, one hand reaching for the weapon under his jacket, but he stumbled and fell to the floor. The women cried out in alarm. Shouts and frantic barking came in through the blasted window. Footsteps pounded away from the door, and then there was a scream.

"Don't let him get away!" someone yelled.

"No!" Tom shouted. "Stay here!" But his voice faltered.

"You're bleeding, Tom!" Ginny cried, bending over him. "Your jacket is all full of holes. Are you all right?"

The noise outside increased as bystanders gathered. Above the human voices, they heard a dog's growl and the pained whimpering of a person in distress. "Okay in there?" someone called.

"Tom's hurt!" Ginny yelled back. "Call the cops and an ambulance!" She slapped her forehead. "*I'll* call them."

A man Tom didn't recognize rushed in, calling Elsie's name. "I'm okay, I'm okay!" she answered him as she fell into his arms. "Oh, Frank, what are you doing here?"

The man's voice was muffled in her hair. "God, Elsie, what is going on? Why is Mike Bingham here?"

Tom managed to sit up and tried to brush away Sue's hands. "Bingham? That was Mike Bingham? Did anyone catch him? Dammit, Sue, I'm okay. Did anyone catch him?"

"We got 'im," said another voice from the door. "The dog's got 'im. He's not going anywhere."

Tom heard Ginny on the phone with the emergency services and Elsie reassuring Frank she wasn't hurt. The name clicked in his head—Frank was Elsie's husband. "Sue, go find out what's going on, would you?" His voice sounded thin and he ached abominably, but though a hundred points of fire seemed to bore into his back, all his systems seemed to be functioning.

Reluctantly, she got to her feet and went to the door. She spoke to someone while a dog growled in the background. Mark Horner, brandishing a large kitchen knife, poked his head in the door. "Don't worry. I'll make sure nobody touches anything until the cops come. You all okay?"

Sue returned to where Tom was still trying to get to his feet. She knelt beside him and he leaned into the support she offered. "Stay where you are," she said. "I can hear sirens, and everything is under control outside."

He felt ghastly. "First day on the job. Never got shot before." He lifted his head. "Is it Mike Bingham?" He waved a hand toward the door.

"I couldn't see. Whoever fired the shot is being held by Maculato and two big men. There's a shotgun on the ground by the window, and our neighbor is watching it. The cops and the EMTs are on the way, so there's nothing for you to do but sit there. You could even faint if you want to."

He turned a pasty smile on her, then lowered his head into his hands. "Cripes, I feel awful."

Chapter Twenty-Five

"I suppose you couldn't ask for better publicity," Tom DiAndreo said to Ginny Brent with a grin. It was a late afternoon in early July and promised to be a fine evening. He sat at Brush & Bevel with the gallery owner and her two employees. There was a lull in the preparations for the festivities surrounding the unveiling of Jerry Berger's last painting, so they enjoyed chowdah in bread bowls before the big event.

Ginny Brent rolled her eyes at him. "Oh, yes I could. Having Jemmie Demarais and Mike Bingham indicted for murder this morning is definitely not good publicity."

Tom laughed, pleased at having teased her. "Sure it is. No such thing as bad publicity, right? You'll get lots of coverage for tonight, and the prints will be in much higher demand because of it, won't they?"

Ginny had to agree to that much. After long discussions, Jenna and Bob Rudolph had agreed to issue a limited edition of two hundred and fifty prints, signed by Howard Berger. After tonight's showing, there would be strong interest.

"In the long run," Elsie Kimball noted, "this messy murder thing won't hurt the art. Especially since we decided to clean off the red stuff once the trial is over." That had taken negotiation, too. Because the watercolor paste—as it turned out to be—was on top of the sealer, it was obviously a late addition, meant only as a clue to the whereabouts of the hidden box of appraisals. It could be removed without compromising the artist's original vision. The prints would be made from the cleaned painting, although they would include a small image of it with the red paste marks and a brief history of the circumstances.

Ginny nodded as if she wasn't sure she agreed. "True. The art is good enough to stand on its own."

Sue Bradley cleared her throat. "How are you feeling, Tom? All healed?"

He moved his arms and twisted his back in demonstration. "All better. Have you guys fixed up all the pellet holes?"

"There weren't that many, really," Ginny told him. "Going through the glass slowed most of the pellets, and the police found the rest on the floor. We found a few more, but nobody was terribly interested in them."

Someone knocked on the front door and flashed a press card. "Seven o'clock!" Sue called. "Not a minute before!"

Ginny sighed. "The phone was so bad I disconnected it. That's what I mean about not good publicity."

"Cheer up," Tom said. "It'll all be over after tonight. Or at least the worst of it will be."

They thought about that for a minute. Then Sue asked, "Would you mind going over it all again, Tom? We know all about how it got from Jerry's studio to here, but everything after that night Mike Bingham showed up is sort of a blur. I'd like to have it all straight in my mind."

The women all turned hopeful eyes to him. He sat

back in his chair—he was still a little sore—and put his thoughts in order. "I have to go back a ways. Some of this isn't confirmed yet, especially the stuff about what happened when Berger and Bingham were killed, so don't talk about it. If anyone asks, just say the police are still looking into it. We still have a lot of questions about a lot of things, but here's what it looks like.

"We think Sue was right, Mike was cheating on insurance and using the money to buy jewelry. It's not entirely clear, but Jemmie seems to be claiming Mike threatened to put frogs in his shop if he didn't comply with his demand for falsified appraisals. As far as we can tell, the frog thing goes all the way back to his childhood. Some pretty nasty hazing, I hear. He was never the most stable character. Anyway, Abby had been a pretty regular customer of Jemmie's until about three months before her death. We don't know how she found out about the scheme, but that's when the appraisals from the other jewelers are dated. Okay so far?"

"So Abby confided in Jerry, and they buried the box out in the woods?" Ginny suggested.

"So it seems. Jerry was smart enough to leave you some clues. There may have been a note that should have come here with the painting. No trace of that ever showed up, but it's mentioned in the receipt from RunAround that we found in his archives. From a few things Jemmie has said when questioned, it looks like Jerry and Abby had a little warning that day. They did the best they could. I wish they had called the cops," he said with regret. "We could have helped. Anyway, Jemmie swears Mike killed Abby, and Mike swears Jemmie killed Jerry. Neither one of them will say anything else about what happened."

Sue snorted. "Neither one could accuse the other without implicating himself. They framed each other. Neat."

"And they made it look like a murder/suicide," Ginny added. "A triple frame. I would guess Mike was responsible for that. Jemmie just doesn't seem capable."

"That's what the Major Crime Unit thinks," Tom agreed. "We don't actually have a good sequence of events for that day. All the rest seems to fall into place. After the murder, they probably dumped Jerry's car in Lowell or someplace like that, where it would have been stripped or stolen right away. The gun probably went with it. Mike does his frantic husband routine, quits his position as alderman, sells the insurance agency, and moves away. He was the natural suspect, of course, but with all the uncertainty about the time of death, there was no way to pin it on him."

There was another rapping on the door. This time Ginny scrawled a hasty sign, "No admittance until 7 p.m.," and taped it to the window, ignoring the shouted questions of another reporter. When her cell phone rang, she checked its display and declined to answer it. "Go ahead, Tom."

"Well, time passed. Leads petered out. Until that painting showed up here, there was no reason to open the case again."

"Wait a minute," Sue said. "Didn't Mike make an insurance claim on the jewelry? Doesn't that ring a bell somewhere?"

"It might have, except nobody seems to have followed up on it. Apparently, he made a claim against the moving company that hauled his stuff out west. Their insurance handled it. Naturally, they didn't want any publicity about it."

"What happened to the actual jewelry?" Elsie asked.

Tom shrugged. "There are dishonest people who will pay for cheap gold and stones, no questions asked. Once the stuff is disassembled and cut up, it gets real hard to trace it."

"Okay," said Sue. "So the painting shows up here, we find the box, and the whole thing busts wide open again, thanks to you, Tom. What I want to know is, how did Jemmie know to follow us into the woods, and how did Mike know we'd all be here the night you were shot?"

"This part is conjecture, but it holds up pretty well. Jemmie knows we've got the painting, which freaks him out even though he doesn't understand the circumstances. He calls Bingham—it shows up on his phone records. Even though we don't know exactly what Bingham says to him, we think he ordered him to keep an eye on you gals. Then he sees me come racing over here, so he does something really old-fashioned. He listens at the door and finds out we're looking for the rocks where the painting was done. I think he followed us from the time we left here, but he might only have picked us up when we turned onto Jerry's road. As for Bingham, I'm sure he kept an eye on the news from here. Once he heard about Jemmie's arrest, he had to come back and see if he could cover things up. His credit cards show he arrived here the day he shot through the window, so obviously he didn't think things through very well. Whether he planned to hurt anybody or just destroy the painting, we don't know."

"And my husband, lucky fellow, just happens to come over for chowdah, and he brings the dog," Elsie said.

Tom shrugged again. "Hey, sometimes even the cops get lucky."

"Yes, but I'm trying to train a bird dog. Not a guard dog. Not a frog dog!"

This time the rapping came on the interior door at the rear of the shop. Ginny walked over and set her hand on the knob. "What's the password?"

"Nosy gals!" came the response.

She grinned and opened the door to Mark Horner and one of his staff, bearing trays of snacks and sandwiches. "I guess story time is over, folks. Sue, Elsie, back to work."

They jumped up and began to arrange the food on the tables. Tom watched the women as they also set out bottles of champagne in coolers and fussed with the remaining artwork on the walls. He realized then, looking around, that there were no other artists represented in the gallery tonight; it was all Jerry Berger. For a moment he wondered where all the framed pieces had come from, but as he strolled around he noted the small tags next to many of them, as in a museum, stating "Loaned by..." or "From the collection of..." There was an impressive number of original works, as well as prints on paper and on canvas. Perhaps he and Donna could afford one of those, someday.

Precisely at 6:45 p.m., Ginny opened the rear door once more to admit two burly men carrying a surprisingly small flat object, covered with a velvet cloth. The men nodded to Tom as they moved to the large easel in the center of the room and set their burden down on it. Tom had, in fact, recommended the off-duty officers to Ginny, to serve as security for the evening, though with Mike and Jemmie both in custody he wasn't terribly worried. Still, an ounce of prevention, as he said.

Sue appeared at his shoulder. "Well, that's everything. Jenna and Bob will be here in a minute. I wonder if the press is still out back?"

"What do you mean?"

Her eyes were bright with mischief. "Well, we had Yaneque put one of those magnetic signs on her new PT Cruiser, the one that doesn't have her name on it yet. According to the sign, she's from something called 'Security Transport,' and she was supposed to cruise through the parking lot, let everyone get a good look, and then go around back. We figured they'd all follow her there and let your men bring the real painting down from the insurance company upstairs."

"You had it at the insurance company?" he asked in disbelief.

She laughed. "Sure! Your guys brought it over from the Rudolphs' yesterday. Don't worry, it's been under lock and key all the time. Ginny upgraded our security system after Mike was here—"

"Thanks for the advice, by the way!" Ginny called from the other side of the room.

"—the Rudolphs are okay on their end. One of the folks from the Silver Spoon let Yaneque in the garage door, so everything is cool. Any minute now Jenna and Bob will walk in, and then we'll open the doors." She heard one more rap on the rear door and opened it to

Yaneque's grinning face, the gap between her front teeth showing.

"Worked like a charm," she said. "I never had so many men following me! I think one is still caught under the door." She giggled.

Tom checked with the security guys, then found an unobtrusive corner where he could watch everything. Once the doors were opened, he planned to circulate quietly among the guests.

A quiet knock was followed by Pam and Howard Berger and the beaming owners of the painting, Jenna and Bob Rudolph. Bob turned out to be a pleasant-looking man in his forties, handsome enough to be a match for Jenna's polished good looks. Ginny took them in hand and showed them the arrangements for the evening. She introduced them to the two burly men and asked them to stand beside the easel for the moment.

At a signal from Ginny, Elsie and Sue joined her at the front door, twitching their clothes into place. They all looked around one more time, took a deep breath, and opened the door.

Warm, humid air accompanied a rush of people who had been milling around in the parking lot. Collectors of Jerry Berger's work rubbed elbows with representatives of the museums that housed his originals. Art critics from Boston and New York raised their eyebrows at the presence of the blatantly uncultured Matt Baldwin, who shuffled about until he found an unobtrusive spot near the finger sandwiches.

Yaneque's ruse had worked for a time, but the press showed up in short order. They made beelines for the Rudolphs and the Brush & Bevel staff, only to find their questions ignored. Elsie and Sue offered champagne and smiles, but no more. Ginny smiled, too, and said only, "Thank you for coming."

Jenna and Bob hovered near the covered painting, greeting anyone who came within earshot and accepting envious congratulations on their good fortune. "Imagine!" people kept exclaiming. "A real Jerry Berger hanging in a bar!" The Rudolphs just smiled and repeated that the full story would be told for the first time that evening.

After it became apparent everyone who was coming had already arrived, Ginny tapped on a wineglass for attention. The crowded room fell silent. "Thank you all for coming," she began. "This is certainly a festive occasion. Tonight Brush and Bevel is pleased to present the first public viewing of *Lady in the Wood*, a formerly unknown work by Jerry Berger, who as you know died about ten years ago. The story of how this piece was lost and recovered will be told for the first time. First, however..." She gestured. "Jenna and Bob, will you do the honors, please?"

With a practiced flourish, the couple removed the dark green velvet veil from the painting. The assembled crowd gave a collective "aah" of appreciation and applauded. They gathered close to view the work in detail. Cameras flashed.

"We have all evening," Ginny continued. "You will have plenty of time to see this wonderful work. Let's start the story with Yaneque Duprey, owner of RunAround Courier Services. Yaneque?"

Rueful grins from the media greeted her as she stepped into the center of the room. Her confidence and rich voice commanded attention. "On a snowy day in December, ten years ago, I picked up a wrapped parcel from Jerry Berger at his studio in Douglass. Unfortunately, a short time later, I was involved in a serious accident in the Temple Pass. When I regained consciousness three days later, I had lost all memory of that day. My memory is still fragmented; however, I do have a receipt from the estate of Mr. Berger that proves I made a pickup from him that day." She laid the yellowed paper on the small table next to the painting and stepped back into the audience.

Ginny named Chris Moran next. A small, tidy gentleman in his late sixties stepped forward. "In the spring of the next year, I was part of a work crew of Rotarians that cleaned up trash in the Pass twice a year. Among the things I found was a clipboard with some nearly dissolved paper and a parcel wrapped in paper and bubble wrap. The paper fell off when I lifted it up. Inside the bubble wrap was a painting. This very one." He indicated the Berger. "I don't know much about art, but I do know what I like." He smiled, earning a laugh. "I took it home and then to my summer place on Cape Cod. My wife didn't like it though, so I took it to my favorite watering hole, Cap'n Billy's." He nodded to Matt Baldwin, who took a few hesitant steps forward, looking to Ginny for encouragement.

"I'm a bahkeepah, not a public speakah," he began in his strong accent. "I owned Cap'n Billy's for yeahs, and one night Chris theah come in and says, 'My wife don't like this. Put it up over the bah and I'll come visit my girlfriend every night.' That's what he called that painting, 'my girlfriend.' So I hung it up and left it theah. Then when I decided to sell out, well, Chris, he hadn't been around for a while, so I sold the girlfriend with the bah. And, well, that's my story." He hastened to the back of the room and caught up his drink with relief.

Next was Jack Morgan, looking more brushed up than Tom would have expected from Ginny's description of her phone call with him. "I bought Cap'n Billy's from Matt about three-four yeahs ago. The painting was theah the whole time I was. After a while I wanted to retire, so I sold the bah and put the furnishings up for auction. The picture, too." He paused and looked at it more closely. "It sure looks a whole lot better all cleaned up and framed."

Bob Rudolph took up the story next. "My part in this is pure serendipity. I work on the Cape now and then, and I used to like going to Cap'n Billy's when I was there. I'd sit at the bar and look at the Lady—well, I was single then, so why not? When I heard it was up for auction, I decided I wanted to have a souvenir of my bachelor days. So I bought it to put in our home here in Westford. My wife Jenna decided to get the painting cleaned up, and she brought it to Brush and Bevel."

Ginny returned to the center of the room. "I was a friend and agent of Jerry's for a long time, and I still serve his estate when it comes to reproductions of his work. When Jenna brought this piece in, I recognized his style, and once my wonderful staff had cleaned up the painting, we found Jerry's signature to confirm it. So here we are with this lovely gift from the past. Isn't it beautiful?" She led another round of applause. As it died down she continued, "But a strange thing happened. There was this line of red dripping from the model's hand. It turned out to be watercolor paste, added on top of the varnish Jerry always used to finish his works. We didn't understand what it meant. It was unlike anything I'd ever seen in any of his work and it troubled me. Then my employee Elsie Kimball was out in the woods near Douglass, training her bird dog Maculato. She found these rocks." She pointed to them, and Elsie spoke up.

"My coworker Sue Bradley and I went out to confirm they were the same rocks as in the painting. At the same time Mr. Berger—Howard, I mean—found a photo in Jerry's archives showing Abby Bingham posing in the rocks. We really went to confirm this was the site where the painting was made. But something else happened."

Without waiting for an introduction, Sue took up the narrative. "While we were there, we found some little red stones under the alder bush that you can see painted in the right hand section of the picture. Officer DiAndreo was with us, and we dug up an old cash box buried under the bush."

"Inside the box were some appraisals," Tom said, actually relieved to finally be sharing his piece of the story. "Based on those appraisals, the model's former husband and a jeweler were indicted today for the murder of Jerry Berger and Abby Bingham. Those of you who were in court today," he looked at several of the reporters, "already know as much as we do about the case."

Despite the questions being called out, Ginny said firmly, "But tonight is a celebration of this beautiful work by an artist we all loved. We cannot talk about the court case, but we can enjoy the last painting Jerry Berger ever completed. Bob and Jenna, we thank you so much for sharing it with us. And we can also announce two things." Her ringing voice silenced the hum in the room. "Jenna and Bob have agreed to a limited edition printing of this work, to be issued once the legalities are complete. Proceeds from the prints will go toward a fund for art education in the local schools. That is very generous. Thank you."

Bob and Jenna blushed and smiled as they received another round of applause.

"And finally," Ginny said, "when they are ready to part with the *Lady in the Wood*, it will become the property of the Sullivan Museum in Mill Falls, where it will be available for viewing forever. Thank you one last time, and thank you to the Sullivan for their help in making it all possible. Now, please enjoy yourselves. Help yourselves to food and drink. Elsie, Sue, and I will be here to answer any questions we can."

Ginny stepped to Tom's side as most of the crowd surged forward to look at the painting. Several of the reporters, however, hovered near her, Elsie and Sue, trying to get more information. The women readily answered questions about identifying and cleaning the painting, but refused all questions about the murders. Finally one reporter closed his notebook and muttered, "From what I heard, it was a really nasty little frame."

Sue nudged Tom with her elbow and nodded toward the *Lady*, where Jenna and Bob stood proudly and possessively with their hands on the wide gold moulding. Her lips twitched and Tom leaned in to hear her.

"Actually," she declared, her head held high, "it's a gorgeous big frame. Brush and Bevel can frame anything!"

A word about the author...

Nikki Andrews has worked as a picture framer, craft store clerk, and administrative assistant, but in her real life she is a writer, editor, and songmaker. She is a member of Talespinners and the New Hampshire Writers Project, and has published two science fiction novels and several short stories. When she's not at her desk, she might be releasing salmon fry on the Piscataquog River, making jams or sweaters, or exploring her surroundings on foot, bike or snowshoe. She lives near a waterfall in New Hampshire with her wonderful husband, a possessive cat, and assorted wildlife.

Nikki enjoys hearing from readers, so contact her at http://www.scrivenersriver.blogspot.com

Thank you for purchasing
this publication of The Wild Rose Press, Inc.
For other wonderful stories of romance,
please visit our on-line bookstore at
www.thewildrosepress.com.

For questions or more information
contact us at
info@thewildrosepress.com.

The Wild Rose Press, Inc.
www.thewildrosepress.com

To visit with authors of
The Wild Rose Press, Inc.
join our yahoo loop at
http://groups.yahoo.com/group/thewildrosepress/

www.ingramcontent.com/pod-product-compliance
Lightning Source LLC
Chambersburg PA
CBHW060932180626
46817CB00004B/1504